The Adventure
of the Treacherous Trust

A New Sherlock Holmes Mystery

Note to Readers:

Your enjoyment of this new Sherlock Holmes mystery will be enhanced by re-reading the original story that inspired this one —
The Adventure of the Bruce-Partington Plans.
It has been appended and may be found in the back portion of this book.

The Adventure of the Treacherous Trust

A New Sherlock Holmes Mystery

Craig Stephen Copland

Published by:

Conservative Growth Inc.

3104 30th Avenue, Ste. 427

Vernon, British, Columbia

Cover design by Rita Toews

ISBN: 9798688974348

Dedication

To the memory of Rev. Mark Buntain who, with his wife, Huldah, founded and directed the Calcutta Mission of Mercy. The mission grew into a large, multi-faceted social service organization that continues to provide aid to thousands of the world's poorest children and families. I was privileged to encounter Mark and Huldah on many occasions during the years I worked in the field of humanitarian aid.

Contents

Acknowledgments

All of us who write pastiche mysteries of Sherlock Holmes owe an everlasting debt to Arthur Conan Doyle, who gave the world the characters and stories of Sherlock Holmes and Dr. Watson. This story is a tribute to *The Adventure of the Bruce-Partington Plans* and is the 42nd in the series.

While we lived in Buenos Aires, I was part of the English Writers Group of that city and enjoyed the weekly meetings where we shared our work and helped each other improve our writing. When we departed Argentina, with regret I left that wonderful group of people. When the COVID pandemic struck, the group moved online and several of us who were no longer living in Buenos Aires joined up again. They have endured numerous chapters of this story and made invaluable suggestions, Thank you.

The Vernon Writers Critique Group also read several chapters of the story and made many very useful corrections and edits. So, thanks to them too.

My older brother, Dr. James Copland and my wife, Mary Engelking are my two finest editors and encouragers. They read and helped improve this story. Thanks.

Mr. Marvin Bethune of Davidson, North Carolina is one of my regular readers, and he bravely offered to let me model one of the characters on him. He is a retired attorney who practiced law for many years in Charlotte, NC and has forebears who came to America from the Isle of Skye. He is an avid fan of Davidson College Wildcats basketball team. Thank you, sir.

The 43rd New Sherlock Holmes Mystery is now being created and is a tribute to *The Adventure of the Devil's Foot*. Plot and character suggestions are always welcome.

Chapter One

A Rooftop in Leatherhead

Everybody who had ever laid eyes on Miss Isabella Cecily Westbury agreed that she was one of the most beautiful young women in London. Her rich auburn hair, perfectly balanced green eyes, slender nose, and alabaster complexion caused both men and women to stop and admire her as she passed them on the pavement.

Everyone who had ever met and conversed with Miss Isabella Cecily Westbury knew why she was loved and adored. Even a brief chat with her always left people feeling better about themselves. She had the gift of encouragement and distributed it liberally to all, from the high and mighty to the bereaved and downtrodden. She volunteered her time and skills at Dr. Barnardo's homes for both boys and girls. The boys, being boys, all fell hopelessly in love with her, and the girls, being girls, all admired and idolized her.

Nobody could say a bad word against her.

Nobody could imagine that her tragic death from a fall off a roof terrace of an estate home in Leatherhead had been anything but a terrible accident.

Nobody thought for even a second that she might have been murdered.

Nobody, that is except her sister, Miss Violet Westbury.

"Mr. Holmes," Miss Violet said whilst sitting in the front room of 221B Baker Street, "my sister was not a clumsy oaf. She was a brilliant dancer, always the best in the class. As children, she and I would have contests walking along railway rails to see who could stay on the longest without falling off. She always won, and she would do it with her eyes closed. For her to lose her balance standing on a chair and watering hanging flower baskets and then fall over the balustrade beggars belief."

My heart went out to this slender, white-faced young lady. Only ten months ago, in November of 1895, she had suffered the loss of her fiancé, the promising young clerk, Mr. Cadogan West. He had, as you will recall from my account of his tragedy, been brutally murdered, his body desecrated and dumped on the top of a railway carriage. Now her life was again laid low by the death of her sister and dearest friend. Her tears betrayed her turmoil as she tried to state her case.

"My deepest sympathy and condolences," I said, "on the loss of your sister. The two of you must have been very close to each other."

"Thank you, Doctor, we were," she said between sobs. "We were only six months apart, and we grew up together. We did everything together."

Then she turned to Holmes.

"It makes no sense, Mr. Holmes," she said after getting control of herself. "My sister could not care a fig for flowers except for ones that came from the florist. She could not tell if a plant was desiccated or drowning. She could hardly tell a petunia from a potato. Izzy would never have taken it upon herself to water a basket of flowers. Never."

I handed her my handkerchief, and she buried her face in it. Holmes waited, not entirely patiently, and continued his questions.

"What was your sister doing in Leatherhead?"

"She was attending the quarterly meeting of the directors of a charitable trust. She had been invited onto the Board of Directors back in December, and they were meeting over a weekend at the estate of the President of the Board."

"His name please?"

"Lord Peter Dalgingham."

"Peter, you say? I know of Lord Bedford Dalgingham."

"That was his father. He died during this past summer, and Peter acquired the estate. Izzy had visited a few times before and thought it was a wonderful place. She so looked forward to the weekend ... and now she is dead. Oh, Mr. Holmes, I know that someone did this to her. I just know it. I know it!"

Tears were streaming down her attractive face, and her fists were clenched. She dabbed her tears with my handkerchief as she struggled to control her feelings. Holmes allowed a few seconds to pass and then posed more questions.

"I know this is very difficult for you," he said, "but you must be absolutely frank with me. Had there been any conflicts of late in your sister's life? Any problems with suitors? Jealousies? Indiscretions? You must be forthcoming even if it is embarrassing to do so."

"No. Nothing. She did not have an enemy in the world. Suitors? Not less than a hundred. She attracted them like flowers attract bees. There was one man, a bit older, who was also on the charity board, that fancied her, and she enjoyed his company. She was quite looking forward to social times with him over the weekend, but it was far from being serious. And she had an invitation for dinner and the theater the following weekend with another fellow. There was no animosity anywhere."

"What charity?"

"The Society for the Care of Street Orphans. It has been in the press all year long. They do wonderful work caring for abandoned children in Calcutta. She was so thrilled to be asked to be a part of it. Oh, please, Mr. Holmes, can you please try and find out what happened to her?"

"I will do my best to help you, Miss Violet. If a vile crime has been committed, I will see that justice is done. However, I must warn you that if I conclude that your sister's death was indeed an accident, tragic though it may have been, I will tell you so. You must prepare your heart for either result. Are you willing to accept that condition?"

She nodded and slowly stood up. I called out for Mrs. Hudson, who quickly appeared, assessed the situation, and helped the young woman on with her coat, led her down the stairs, and found her a cab to take her home.

"Well, Holmes," I said once the two of us were alone, "you do not appear overly eager to take this case on. I detect reservations."

He lit his pipe and took a few puffs before responding.

"Heartbreaking accidents, unfortunately, do happen. Even the most agile of football players occasionally trip and fall whilst crossing the street. Given the treacherous events that led to the death of Cadogan West, it is not surprising that Miss Westbury would doubt the first report of the local police. Evil can lurk in the most unsuspected places, but philanthropists of respected charities are not known for tossing young women off terraces to their death. So, yes, I do indeed have reservations."

"What are you going to do?"

"You remember Inspector Baynes of the Surrey Constabulary?"

"Of course. Quite a good man. One of the brighter police inspectors you have worked with. Looking into a death in Leatherhead would have fallen into his bailiwick, would it not?"

"Indeed. I'll send off a wire to him, asking for his insights. If he is entirely assured that it was no more than an accident, I shall not waste my time taking the matter any further."

Holmes wrote out a note and, descending to Baker Street, summoned a bicycle boy to take it to the post office and have it telegraphed to Surrey. Then he returned to his chemical table and lit his Bunsen burner. He settled into an experiment that would likely take several hours to complete, and I attended to writing up my account of a case that had been concluded the previous week.

Neither of us got very far. Two hours later, a knock came to the door, and a telegram was delivered, a very fast reply from the office of the Surrey Constabulary. It ran:

Mr. Holmes: Thankful you have been brought into this matter. Was about to contact you myself. If possible, could you come to constabulary office Woking tomorrow? Some issues with this accidental death beyond me. Baynes.

Holmes read the telegram and then looked over at me.

"Watson?"

"Right, Holmes. Shall be ready to depart tomorrow morning."

Chapter Two

Five Smooth Stones

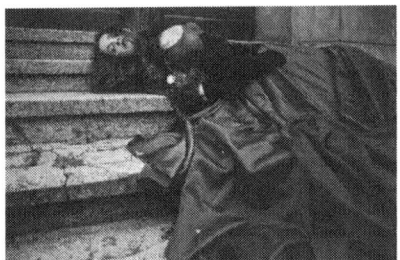

The following day, just after dawn, we took a cab to Victoria and boarded the first train to Sussex. Once settled into our cabin, I opened the newspaper to see if there was anything about the death of Miss Westbury. To my disappointment, there was nothing. As there was an election campaign taking place in America, the English press was obsessed with their haughty opinions on the colony that got away. The snobs of Fleet Street were, as one would expect, looking down their noses on the fellow from a small town in Illinois, Mr. William Jennings Bryan, who was stomping around the country admonishing the populace not to "crucify mankind on a cross of gold." It occurred to me that the Brahmins and Knickerbockers had so soon forgotten the legacy of the long-legged backwoods lawyer, also from Illinois.

I put the paper aside and posed a question to Holmes.

"Violet Westbury's family," I said, "must not have been traditional. Six months between her and her sister. Were you aware of that?"

"Yes. I had made inquiries about her last year in connection with the death of Cadogan West. Her father died just before she was born, and her mother remarried two years later to a widower who also had an infant daughter. They became one happy family."

"Are both parents still living?"

"The step-father was somewhat older and passed away. Her maternal grandfather, also a widower, lived with them and assumed the role of a devoted father. He and the mother, his daughter, raised the two girls."

"A wealthy family? Middle-class? Struggling?"

"Quite well off," said Holmes. "The grandfather, a Mr. Harris Paterson, was a poor Scot who migrated to London and apprenticed to a butcher. Over time, with talent and very hard work, he opened his own shop, and then several more. His entire family worked together in the business. By the time he retired and sold his chain of meat shops, he was a moderately wealthy man. The girls had to work in the family enterprise, but they were not deprived."

"Ah, that is good to know." I felt some comfort knowing that Miss Violet had a mother and grandfather to help her through her year of loss. At least she would not be wanting for financial security, and there was something to be said for that.

"There is one other piece of data," Holmes added, "that I learned about her. The grandfather had taken out a life insurance policy on her. Miss Violet and the mother were the beneficiaries."

We lapsed into silence and were only fifteen minutes out of Woking when Holmes asked a question of me.

"What do you know about this charity?"

"Only what I read in the press," I said. "They have been in the papers constantly for the past year. They are by far the most popular charity of the season. Everyone, from the toffs to the working men and women, seems to want to do their bit to help them."

"What do they do?"

"They rescue abandoned children from the streets of Calcutta and place them in orphanages. They teach them a trade and put them to work."

"There must be a score of charities that all do the same thing in cities all over the globe. Why are they so attractive to the British public?"

"They have a flair for promotion. The founders, Peter Dalgingham and Timothy Olleitch, spent a month in India on a mission excursion and then wrote a book about the vision God had given them for rescuing children."

"Oh, yes," said Holmes, "I see that book in all the bookstores. *Three Cups of Rice* or something like that, isn't it?"

"That's it. All it takes is three cups of rice to keep a child in India adequately fed for a week. That much rice can be had for a pittance. Even a common working man can send in a shilling or two a month and know that he is saving a poor child who might otherwise starve."

"Very clever. And the response?"

"Overwhelming. Tens of thousands of people are sending in their shillings."

Inspector Baynes was waiting for us at the Woking station and led us to the Sussex Constabulary office a block away. After a brief chat, a cup of tea and some warm scones, he came to the case.

"I said, Mr. Holmes, that I was thankful you were working on the case as there is something about it that just does not feel right. And, sir, I know you demand that a detective depend on science, facts, and logical deductions and not on feelings. So, I must admit that I am somewhat hesitant—embarrassed might be a better word—to admit to you that I have no hard evidence, but I smelt a fish. I have this feeling and—,"

"No, no, no," interrupted Holmes. "There is nothing at all wrong with trusting your preliminary feelings. I do it all the time. What we call our intuition, our uneasy response to initial data, is not nonsense at all. It is our insight based on data that we have not yet completely assembled and organized in our minds. There is always a reason for our so-called feelings. The only problem is that we have not yet been able to find a satisfactory explanation. By all means, Inspector, divulge your feelings and pray, do not hesitate to add any detail, illogical though it may appear at this time."

"Oh, well. Thank you, Mr. Holmes. Thank you. Very well, I will tell you everything I know and try to put into words what a voice inside me is saying. But first, let me give you the report and let me draw your attention to the record of the interviews of the staff conducted by one of my men."

He had prepared two copies of the incident report and handed one to each of us. Holmes thumbed through the pages quickly and suggested an alternative.

"It would make the most efficient use of the hour it will take us to go to Leatherhead, Inspector, if we were to embark straight away and peruse this report on route. Might that be possible, sir?"

"Jolly good idea."

We clambered into a police wagon and set out on the road from Woking to Leatherhead.

It took a full twenty minutes for us to read the report from start to finish, and my only conclusion was that it was what one might expect of competent, diligent policemen who were neither rushed nor careless in completing their paperwork.

"Does anything," Inspector Baynes asked us, "strike you as questionable?"

"The watering can," said Holmes.

"Ah ha! I knew you would spot it. Thank you, Mr. Holmes. You see, I've learned a thing or two from you over the years."

"The watering can?" I said. "It says that it landed beside her. What was odd about it? If she was watering the flowers, you could hardly expect she would have set it down before falling?"

"My dear Watson," said Holmes, "kindly read that portion of the report to us."

I flipped back through the pages and found the report of the local constable who had interviewed a Miss Edith Smoot, the maid. It ran:

Miss Smoot was the first person to arrive at the site of the incident. She said she was the maid. She said she had been dusting and cleaning the parlor. A window was open. She said she was sure it was just after six o'clock because she always starts her evening parlor duty at six and had just finished fluffing the pillows and dusting the busts of Charles Darwin and Napoleon on the mantle. She said she heard a terrible scream and then a thud. She said the scream was very loud and came from outside the window. The thud was followed a few seconds later by a loud 'clank' (her word), a metallic sound. That metallic sound was followed by several other metallic sounds, but not as loud. She rushed to the window and saw Miss Westbury lying on the flagstone pavement. She rushed out of the building and came to where the lady was lying. Her head was at a 'real odd' (her words) angle. A metal watering can lay about ten feet away. The woman was still breathing, and her eyes were open. For a second, the maid said it looked like the woman was trying to say something. But then she stopped breathing. The maid checked her neck for a pulse but could tell that it was broken, and there was no pulse.

"You can stop there," said Holmes.

"Why? There was nothing odd in what I read?" I said.

Holmes sighed, rolled his eyes, and gave me a familiar and condescending smile.

"I shall explain it later. Now then, Inspector, please tell us what you know about the men who were present at the time of the accident."

"Right. So, about these charity chaps. There were five directors. Four men and Miss Westbury. And then there is the General Secretary, Mr. Olleitch. He is an American but was sent to England for his schooling. I have only some preliminary details, but here's what I have. All these fellows were in the same year at Harrow, and they all played on the same rugby team. Now there's nothing wrong with a group of friends getting together to do good deeds but—and here I'm on shaky ground—they didn't strike me as the type that cared about the poor and starving off in India. They seemed rather snobbish about being British, if you know what I mean."

"I do," said Holmes, "but the woman was inclined toward charity, was she not?"

"Right, Sir. And for the life of me, I don't know how she came to be on the board. It is quite irregular for a woman to serve as a director. Maybe they wanted the appearance of being enlightened and all."

"Quite possibly," said Holmes. "No doubt there exists a complete explanation. We simply do not know what it is. Not yet."

Baynes opened his notebook and started to chat whilst Holmes sat as still as a statue, his eyes closed.

"All of these directors and the general secretary come from fine, respected families. Two from England, one from Wales, one from Scotland and the American"

"All Christian families?"

"I did not think to check on that, but I assume so."

"Well, are any of them Jews?" said Holmes.

"No. At least none going by their names and faces."

"Any Catholics?"

"I did not think to ask about that. Would that make a difference?"

"Sometimes. I assume that none came from India. None with dark skin."

"None. All quite the handsome lot. Jolly good athletes."

"Interesting. Pray, continue."

"All of them claim to have been together in the library when the fall took place. We gave everyone the third degree, but their stories were consistent, down to the last detail of time and place and action that took place up to when the maid rushed in screaming about Miss Westbury."

"How very curious."

"That's what I thought as well, Mr. Holmes. I had this feeling that I was being lied to, but they are a very clever lot. All went to a public school and then on to either Oxford or Cambridge, except for one who went to the Sorbonne. Try as I might, I could not trip them up on anything … but … I had this feeling that they were lying."

"Perhaps they were. You have excellent instincts for a young police inspector. So, perhaps we are about to embark on a challenging investigation. I was very impressed with your work at Wisteria Lodge, and I look forward to assisting you again."

"Oh, come now, Mr. Holmes. It will be me who is assisting you."

"Not at all. I have no need to enhance my reputation. You have a promising career in front of you. It will be a pleasure to do whatever I can to help."

The inspector rattled on about the charity directors as we drove to Leatherhead. All of the men were in their early thirties, all married to highly suitable wives, and all were employed and doing well in commerce, the City, industry, or Her Majesty's government. Not a single mark against any of them.

Holmes listened, eyes closed, nodding from time to time.

When we arrived at the gate of the Dalgingham estate, Holmes insisted that we stop, get out, and walk into the property.

"It is easier to make observations when walking," he said. "Sometimes, you can see quite a lot just by looking. For example, the nameplate on the gate post has only been put in place recently."

I walked over and took a close look at it. The small, gleaming brass plate read *Five Smooth Stones.*

"An odd new name to give an old estate," I said. "Does the new owner have delusions of killing giants with a slingshot?"

"Perhaps he only imagines himself a perfect man, standing in a museum in Florence, adored by the multitudes," said Holmes.

The driveway wound through a small stand of trees before opening on a wide expanse of lawns. Holmes stopped there and took out his spyglass. On the flat lawn adjacent to the manor house, I could see four boys with a wicket set up and practicing their cricket.

"What are they doing here?" I asked Baynes.

"They're with the charity. There are sixteen in all, eight boys and eight girls. They brought them here from Calcutta. They hold these big public lectures and spectacles where they sing and perform, and they're quite good at it. And then a few of them give their testimonies telling the audience all about the horrors of their life before being rescued by the good people from the Society. The stories are said to bring a tear to the eye of even the hardest miner or foundry worker."

"And, no doubt," said Holmes, "a donation from their pockets. But these boys are of interest to me for more than that."

He had not stopped observing the lads playing cricket and continued doing so for another full five minutes.

"Holmes," I said, "is there something wrong with them?"

"Wrong? No, there is nothing wrong with them at all. They are all handsome and are excellent young athletes."

I knew the look on his face.

"Then what is the issue you have with them?"

"It is entirely too early," he said while still looking, "to post any warning, but we have come here in part because there is some reason to suspect that these men might possibly have brought about the death of the young woman. Would you agree, gentlemen?"

Both Inspector Baynes and I mumbled our agreement.

"My issue, Watson, is that any men who would risk committing the murder of a young English woman whose family and friends have access to the police, to me, and to the press, would not hesitate to kill an orphan child from the streets of Calcutta if it was expedient for their purposes."

"What are you saying, Mr. Holmes?" asked the inspector.

"Only that these children may not be safe."

Chapter Three

Madder Than a Wet Hen

The lawns and gardens were beautifully laid out and cared for. Small trees and shrubs gave evidence of recent improvements, and the air bore the occasional whiff of a stable of horses somewhere not too far away. The house itself was gleaming white and had been given a fresh coat of paint earlier that year. The spots of paint on the window sills and the bordering pavement and gardens that even the most careful of painters leave behind were still evident.

We had approached the house in silence with the result that no groom had rushed out to hold the horses, and no maid or butler had heard us and already opened the door. A friendly but firm knocking by Inspector Baynes brought a young maid to the entrance.

"Good morning, Inspector Baynes," said the plain but pleasant-looking young maid. "We were not told you were returning. Do come in."

"Good morning, Miss Edith. Please tell his Lordship that I have come back for another visit and have brought Mr. Sherlock Holmes with me. We need to have a brief word with him."

Her eyes went wide on hearing the name of Sherlock Holmes.

"Are you really Sherlock Holmes? Oh, I can't wait to tell the rest of the staff that we have the famous detective here. They will all want to meet you, Mr. Holmes. Can I—,"

"Edith," said Baynes. "I'm sorry, but we do not have time for that, please call his Lordship and ask him to come."

"Oh, come now, Inspector," said Holmes, "of course, we have time. There is no rush. Miss Edith, why don't you let the staff all know that both Dr. Watson and Sherlock Holmes are here and tell them that we would be delighted to meet them all for a chat and a cup of tea in the kitchen. Lord Dalgingham can wait. Now, off you go, my girl and round up the gang."

I was surprised by Holmes's violation of established protocol when calling on a member of the nobility, but I knew him well enough not to question his unorthodox behavior.

Five minutes later, Holmes and I sat down in the kitchen with the chambermaid, a cook, a butler, a gardener, a young groom, and a semi-toothed grisly fellow who must have been a general maintenance factotum and caretaker. Holmes cheerfully took out his calling cards, signed the back of them, and gave one to each of the staff. They looked like children who had just opened their stockings on Christmas morning, and the atmosphere around the table became rather convivial.

"It's terribly good of you to come together for me," said Holmes. "Is this the entire staff? There are surprisingly few of you."

"We used to be more," said Edith. "But what with His Lordship—the father, that is—passing away, it was not the same as it had been for all those years. A few gave their notice and went to look for new situations. For some, it was time for a change."

"Completely understandable," said Holmes. "Now, I shan't keep you long from your tasks, but I do need your help on what it was that brought me here to Five Smooth Stones."

"Owww, don't be calling it that," said the cook. "That's the name that Lord Peter give it a few months back. To us, it will always be Linden Hill. That's what His Lordship, bless him, called it, and that's what it will always be to us."

"I stand corrected. Now then, about the reason for my visit."

"It's about Miss Isabella," said the groom.

"It is indeed."

"If I may say something, Mr. Holmes," said the butler. "My name is Bentley Fulbright, and I supervised the staff under His Lordship and continue to do so under his son. I am quite thrilled to have you chat with us, but I am afraid I must remind you that all of us in service have made a promise to guard the confidence of our employer, even if we are not terribly fond of him."

His statement brought a smirk or two from his colleagues, and a roll of the eyes from two others.

"And I would never for a moment," said Holmes, "dream of putting good people in a situation that would lead them to violate their promise. My only interest is in Miss Isabella herself. Kindly, let me explain. The young woman was the sole future support of her widowed mother and her grandfather. He, being a prudent old butcher, took out a life insurance policy on his granddaughter, ensuring that in the unlikely event of anything happening to her, there would be sufficient funds available for the care of her mother and sister. The problem, as I am sure you must know, is that such insurance policies, especially when placed on the lives of young women, are declared null and void in the event that a death is self-inflicted."

"You mean suicide? You mean if Miss Isabella jumped from the terrace to kill herself?" said the groom.

"Precisely. You, the staff of this house, had the opportunity to observe Miss Westbury all last weekend whilst she was here. All I need to know from you is whether or not she showed any signs of being horribly sad. Did she do anything that might have led you to worry about the state of her heart and mind?"

"Only on this visit?" asked the maid. "She was here back three months ago, and once before that, before Christmas."

"Ah, was she? Very well then, on any of her three visits?"

"I can answer that," said the cook. "I'm Bertha Johnson, and this is my kitchen, so I can tell you that on her first two visits, Miss Izzy— that was what she told us to call her—would come in here after every meal and thank me and the rest of us for the splendidly fabulous meal—that was her words, every time—we had prepared. She was like a ray of sunshine. Made our day, she did."

"And last weekend?" said Holmes.

"She didn't come in. Not once. And it wasn't the food."

"Aye," said Edith. "It was the same with the maids. She used to stop and chat and give us a good word. But this time, it was as if she was on another planet. Walked past me all the time like I wasn't there."

"Something must have upset her," said Holmes. "Can any of you possibly enlighten me as to what it might have been."

"Please, Mr. Holmes," said the butler. "How can anyone know what is going on in the mind of a pretty young woman? For me, that continent is *terra incognita,* as I am sure it is for all of us."

"Like hell, it is!"

This came from the maintenance chap, who stood up and looked directly at Holmes.

"We all know what was eating her up."

"Evan!" said the butler. "That is enough. We have a duty—"

"You do, Bentley. I don't. You're employed here in service, but I punch my own ticket and bill my hours every week, and that's what I get paid for. So, I'm not violating any promise, and if I never work another day for Master Peter, I won't miss it. So, I'll tell you about her this past weekend. She was madder than a wet hen, she was. We all saw that. Now, didn't we?"

He directed his last question to those around him. I detected a few very shallow nods of agreement.

"At whom was she angry?" asked Holmes. "Anyone in particular?"

All of the heads turned to Evan.

"At Master Peter. Every one of us overheard them having words in the dining room or in the hall. And you heard them during the meeting, didn't you Edith, when you brought in the tea?"

Edith directed her gaze to the carpet, but her faint nod and biting her lip could not be missed.

"Did any of you," asked Holmes, "happen to overhear what they were arguing about?"

"She wanted to see something," said Evan, "and he wouldn't show it to her. We all heard them, and we've all talked about it here in the kitchen, but none of us know what it was."

"I do." This came from the young groom, and all now eyes turned and looked at him.

"And your name, please, young man?" said Holmes.

"Arnold, Mr. Holmes. Arnold Ballard. And I can tell you that after their meeting on Saturday afternoon, they had two hours off before dinner. She came over to the stable and asked if I could saddle up a horse for her to take out for a ride. What she says was, 'Master, Arnold'—she always called me that. She treated me with respect, she did. She did that for all of us—'would you so kind as to pick out a strong mount for me. I need to go for a jolly good gallop to blow off some steam.' So, I go and fetch Queen Tabitha—she's a big, spirited mare—and get her ready, and Miss Isabella hops up on her like a true rider, but then the mare starts getting skittish. And so, I says, 'Miss, you will have to relax yourself. A horse can always tell when her rider is on edge, and Queen Tabitha knows that you are wound up tighter than a drum.' Well then, she looks and me and smiles, and she says, 'Sir, if you could promise to do something for me, something that may require stealth and maybe even some danger, I would be able to relax and enjoy my ride.' Well, I couldn't say 'no' to her. I would have done anything—charged into battle, anything. She was like a goddess to me. So, she says, 'Tonight, after it is dark, I want you to go into the library. On the desk is a large ledger bookmarked with this year's date. I want you to bring that book to me up in my bedroom without anyone seeing you. And then to wait inside my bedroom for as long as it takes me to read it and make notes. It may be several hours. And then take it back. Could you do that for me?' Well, I said I could do that, and truth be, I was thrilled to be asked. That's what she was wanting and what Master Peter the Pecker wouldn't let her have."

Every eye in the room was fixed on him as he sat down.

"That was a highly inappropriate request for her to make," said Holmes. "Did you do that?"

"No. I would have. But she came back from her ride just before dinner, and then she was killed by her fall. I was too tied up in knots to think about it, and there was no use anyway what with her being dead."

Holmes was about to say something when a man appeared in the doorway of the kitchen and bellowed at us.

"What is going on here!?"

The accent was distinctly American. I turned to see a tall, slender man of about thirty years of age, well-dressed, and wearing eyeglasses. He did not appear to be at all happy. Holmes turned to him and beamed a wide if insincere grin.

"And good morning to you, sir. My name is Sherlock Holmes, and I am afraid that this impromptu gathering is all my fault. Or, to be more accurate, it is all the fault of my dear colleague, Dr. Watson."

He gestured in my direction in a more than somewhat dramatic fashion. I picked up his cue.

"Me? What do you mean me?"

"It is all because of those sensationalist stories you have written about me, turning me into a dashing hero and causing these good, hard-working people to demand a chance to meet me and have my autograph. Fame is such a tedious burden at times, but one must be kind to the readers, mustn't one?"

Then, turning to the fellow in the doorway, added, "But we will not be much longer, my good man. So kindly run along and let us finish up here."

The American chap directed his sharp reply to the staff. "Every one of you, back to your work. And I suggest that you, Mr. Holmes, leave and make a proper appointment. Good day, sir."

Inspector Baynes, who had been standing quietly in a corner of the kitchen, now strolled over and stood in front of the fellow.

"Allow me to remind you, Mr. Olleitch, that you have no authority in this house. I brought Mr. Holmes here, and you do not give orders to an Inspector of the Surrey Constabulary. Please go and find his Lordship and tell him that I will meet him in the library in five minutes and will be accompanied by Mr. Sherlock Holmes. Please do that now, sir."

The American's face reddened, and he turned and departed. Holmes graciously thanked the staff for their help, and, in return, Mr. Bentley Fulbright thanked him for his generous sharing of his time. Then he turned to his fellow staff members.

"It would be most appropriate if all of us remembered only the pleasure of receiving autographed cards from the famous Mr. Sherlock Holmes and forgot any other conversation that took place. Are we agreed?"

Heads nodded, and the staff departed.

The library was quite well-stocked for a country house. Several portraits of Lord Bedford Dalgingham ringed the upper wall. They began when he was a cavalier young Highlander and progressed through several decades to his final years as a dour auld Scot. There were a few paintings of life under the Raj, and numerous busts of poets, kings, and Roman emperors. A copy of one of the most popular portraits of Her Majesty held a place of honor above the entryway. We had not been in the room for more than a few minutes before a second man entered and strode energetically toward us.

"Why halloa! If it isn't the famous Mr. Sherlock Holmes. What a splendid treat. How can I thank you for coming all the way to Sussex? I'm Peter Dalgingham and, obviously, just delighted to meet you."

Chapter Four

Coincidence or Divine Intervention?

Lord Peter Dalgingham had a strikingly handsome face and brilliant blue eyes. Most of his hair had departed, except for a rust-colored fringe along the sides and back of his head, but his perfectly contoured bald head give him a spiffing masculine look, and he exuded energy and the easy confidence that comes with being born into wealth and having attended only the best of schools.

He came directly to Holmes, extended his hand and shook Holmes's vigorously, adding a grasp of his left hand to Holmes's wrist. He then did the same to me and gave a gracious nod to Inspector Baynes.

"Your arrival," he said to us, "is utterly marvelous. Perfectly fortuitous. Why just this morning over breakfast, Timothy and I were talking about asking you to pay us a visit. Oh, have you met Timothy? He's the General Secretary of our Society. Totally brilliant man, and with such a heart for the children. Do let me have him join us ... TIMOTHY! Can you join us in the library?!"

He directed this shout to the door of the library, and a moment later, the American fellow who minutes before had been visibly angry appeared, smiling pleasantly.

"Timothy, this is Mr. Sherlock Holmes. Oh, yes, you already met him, didn't you? I was about to tell him about our conversation this morning and your splendid suggestion that we invite him to pay us a visit as soon as possible."

"Why would you want me to come here?" said Holmes whilst our host was between breaths.

"Why? Well, it is so important ... not to us ... but to the children we are trying to help. I'm sure you know, Mr. Holmes, that the English public can be terribly fickle. We have been wonderfully blessed with popularity and generous donors who have responded not to any of us but to the children themselves. But all a Society such as ours has to support it ultimately is its good name. Anything that might tarnish our reputation can be devastating to our support, and then, can you imagine what that would do to the children, all those poor boys and girls we have taken off the streets of Calcutta?"

"I assume that you could no longer keep them fed and put them to work."

"Ah, yes, indeed, Mr. Holmes. We encourage every one of them to be industrious. Our motto was borrowed from a wonderful novelist in Germany. *Arbeit macht frei*. In English, that means *work makes you free*. We tell them that over and over. And they respond wonderfully and become like busy little worker bees. Hard work is their ticket to freedom. Would you not agree, Mr. Holmes?"

"That is not my area of expertise. However, I assume that you were worried your homes and shops in Calcutta would be imperiled by the news of the death of Miss Westbury."

"Exactly, sir. After the tragic death of Miss Westbury, we knew we were at risk, and the brilliant suggestion Timothy came up with was to call in Sherlock Holmes and engage his services to carry out a full investigation. Of course, it would clear our name straight away, remove any doubt about the probity of our Society and allow the work to carry on unimpeded. And here you are."

"I accept your request for my services. How very coincidental that I arrived so conveniently."

"Coincidence, Mr. Holmes? We believe in divine intervention. Our prayers have been answered. And we are waiting upon the Lord to answer our other request from this morning."

"Are you now? And what might that have been?"

"We are establishing a special fund and appeal in the name of Miss Isabella Westbury. She had a deep concern, a passion, for helping girls who needed to be rescued from the streets of Calcutta. In honor of her life and her convictions, and after seeking guidance from God, we decided to establish that fund and launch a special appeal. This very morning, we prayed earnestly for a heavenly blessing. Timothy will send out the notices to the press today, and our little choir of God's dark-skinned children, our Chorale of Angels, will give a concert ten days from now in the Royal Albert. I will send a personal invitation to 221B Baker Street, Mr. Holmes, and I do hope you will be able to join us for a splendid ... a sensational event."

"I will mark it on my calendar. Now then, if you truly expect me to carry out a complete investigation and clear your name, I am sure you will not object to my asking a few preliminary questions."

"Oh, why, of course not. No objection, whatsoever. As the directors of a charitable trust, we are an open book, aren't we, Timothy?"

"Indeed, we are," said Mr. Olleitch, the General Secretary. "I trust that Mr. Sherlock Holmes expected nothing less."

"Brilliant. Then let me start with the most obvious anomaly. Why was Miss Westbury a member of your Board of Directors? All of you were old boys from Harrow, yet she was invited to join you back in the fall. Why was that?"

"My father, sir. Dear old Lord Bedford Dalgingham. Bless his heart."

"Your father?"

"Yes, Mr. Holmes. Father, before he went on to his eternal reward, had been one of the directors of the National Incorporated Association for Reclamation of Destitute Waif Children, known by the public as Dr. Barnardo's Homes. He and Dr. Tom Barnardo were dear friends, and he had carried out that role since the Homes were founded. Miss Westbury volunteered faithfully at the Homes and—what can I say, Mr. Holmes? You know how some older men are with exceptionally attractive younger women—she caught his eye, and he took an interest in her—utterly honorable of course—and chatted with her often and took her under his wing, as they say. He wanted to provide her with opportunities to broaden her horizons, and so, he came to me and told me in no uncertain terms that I was to add her to the directors of our Society. I had never met her and knew nothing about her, but I learned as a boy that I disobeyed my father at my peril. So, of course, I invited her to join us. Her presence at our meetings greatly enhanced the atmosphere, and not one of our old boys ever missed a meeting after she joined us. Isn't that so, Timothy?"

"Amen to that," said Mr. Olleitch. "It was a delight to have such a lovely young woman on board."

"If she was such a delight," said Holmes, "why did you exchange harsh words with her on that Saturday afternoon?"

If Holmes's blunt question caught the young baron off guard, I could not tell. There was not even a flicker of hesitation.

"Harsh words, Mr. Holmes?" replied the young lord. "Harsh words, indeed. That, sir, is a gross understatement. To tell you the truth, it would be far more accurate to say that she bit my head off. And did I ever learn a lesson from that one."

"Explain, please."

"It's a mistake I assure you that I will not make again. Miss Westbury had asked to review the miles of financial records of the Society. I told her, without thinking, I admit, that she had no need to worry her pretty little head about all that and that the men, our treasurer, and general secretary, were doing a fine job looking after that. And whoa! Did I ever get a lecture from her. Emancipated young women do not like being told such things, and who can blame them? I assure you, Mr. Holmes, I have learned my lesson."

"And did you then release the records to her?"

"Well, of course, I would have, but the process was interrupted—horribly interrupted—by her tragic death later that afternoon. Otherwise, she could have reviewed them to her heart's content."

"And are you willing to release those records to me as part of my investigation?"

"Why, of course, we are. Can we arrange to do that, Timothy?"

"Certainly. The books are now with our auditors, and they will complete their review within the next month and send their report to the Commissioner for Charities. And then they will be available to you, Mr. Holmes, and to any member of the public who so requests."

"Excellent. I look forward to the opportunity. Now, if I may, I would appreciate your taking me to the terrace from which Miss Westbury fell. Would you mind doing that, sir?"

"I … I would like to … but I … I am so sorry … I just can't. Please, Mr. Holmes … it is just too painful for me. Isabella was such a thing of beauty to all of us … and her death has hit us very hard."

He paused here and took out his handkerchief and dabbed his eyes, and then continued.

"Perhaps, Mr. Olleitch could do that. Could you, Timothy? I know it has been hard on you as well, but you seem to be made of sterner stuff than I am. Would you mind?"

"Certainly, your Lordship," said Mr. Olleitch. "Gentlemen, if you would wait here for a few minutes, I shall have to find our caretaker and get the key to the terrace from him. I am not sure where he is, but I shall find him and be right back. Please, make yourselves comfortable."

He gestured to a sofa and set of reading chairs, turned, and departed. Lord Dalgingham left with him.

Once they were beyond earshot, I looked at Holmes and Inspector Baynes.

"What do you make of them?" I asked.

"They are both Oxford products by way of Harrow," said Holmes. "As such, they are either exceptionally polished and capable pious frauds, or dedicated and diligent philanthropists. Possibly both."

It was a full ten minutes before Mr. Olleitch returned, brandishing a key and seeming somewhat short of breath.

"Sorry for the delay. Please follow me."

We climbed three floors of a central staircase and then a fourth set of narrow ones leading to the roof. Mr. Olleitch opened a small door and led the three of us out onto a roof terrace. It was a pleasant place with several pieces of garden furniture and offered a stunning view of the entire countryside. On two sides of the perimeter of the terrace, sets of posts and lintels supported an array of hanging flower baskets that were overflowing with geraniums, cascading petunias, fuchsias, and several flowers I could not identify. The parade of arches and baskets that faced the front of the house must have been the place from which the tragic fall took place. Holmes walked immediately to the location and leaned over the balustrade. The path of a falling body would have had nothing to hinder it all the way to the ground below.

"From which place along the edge did she fall?" he asked Mr. Olleitch.

"This one," he said, pointing to the section closest to the first corner. "That is where the chair was toppled over, and it lines up with the location of her body on the flagstone below."

"Where is the chair?"

"In the small alcove beside the door."

"And is that one the same chair?"

"Yes, Mr. Holmes."

Holmes walked over to the alcove and looked at the plain metal chair. A watering can sat on the floor beside it.

"And is this the same watering can?"

"Yes."

"How did Miss Westbury obtain the key?"

"The door was open. After the tragedy, His Lordship demanded that the caretaker lock it so that no such event could ever happen again. No one has been on the terrace since then."

"Ah, yes. A wise move," said Holmes, and then he looked out over the front lawn of the estate. "I see that you have a few boys playing cricket on the front lawn. Do they reside in the house?"

"They do."

"And do they ever come up here?"

"They used to. His Lordship has since forbidden them to do so. It is now obvious that it is too dangerous."

"I assume those four boys are members of your Chorale of Angels. Where are the other members?"

"They live in a children's home in London and rotate their stay here at Five Smooth Stones. His Lordship wishes to give all of them an equal opportunity to enjoy the benefits a short stay at the estate has to give them."

"Oh, yes, quite decent of him."

"You are welcome to speak with them if you wish. However, they are all recently arrived from Calcutta and, unlike the staff of the house, will not be your adoring fans."

"Of course not. But no doubt they are yours and His Lordship's. And I believe that is all I need to see for the present. What about you, Inspector, or you, Doctor?"

I shook my head, but Inspector Baynes posed a question.

"Those four boys out on the lawn; they were not the same four children who were here on the weekend. Is that correct?"

"You are correct, Inspector. After the weekend, a new group rotated in."

We descended from the terrace, and Holmes requested an opportunity to speak with Lord Peter Dalgingham. Unfortunately, we were told that he was indisposed at present but could arrange an appointment the following day. With no further access to the staff, we departed.

As we pulled out of the driveway and started back to Woking, Holmes suddenly leaned his head out of the window of the carriage and called for the driver to stop.

"I see the gardener just off the drive," he said to Baynes and me. "I need to have a word with him."

He returned five minutes later.

"Mind if I ask, Mr. Holmes," said the inspector, "why you wanted to see him?"

"To ask about the watering of the flower baskets. He assured me that he tends to them first thing every morning when the terrace is dry, but the grass and shrubs are still wet from the dew."

As we neared the station in Woking, Baynes pressed Holmes for his insights.

"Data, my dear Inspector," said Holmes. "We know too little. So early in the game, we must resist the temptation to form a hypothesis based on preliminary knowledge. The explanations given are not without reason and plausibility. Is it possible that an athletic young woman, whilst angry, took herself up to the terrace, and once there, decided to water the baskets with a nearly empty watering can, fell off the spotlessly clean chair, and toppled over the balustrade? Yes, it is possible."

"But is it likely?" I asked.

"Of course not. But I can recount a hundred cases where the final solution did not appear at the outset to be the likely one. Until we know more, our minds will remain open."

The inspector was silent for several minutes as if he needed some time to absorb Holmes's comments. When we stopped in front of the station, he posed a final question.

"What are you going to do now, Mr. Holmes?"

"Dr. Watson and I shall pay a visit to the bereaved family. Tomorrow morning."

Once inside our train cabin, I could not contain my curiosity.

"Holmes, explain this issue with the watering can."

"My dear Watson, in the incident report, did you not notice the words 'a few seconds.' There was a period of time between the thud of the body hitting and the metallic sound of the watering can. If you were standing on a chair beside a balustrade holding a watering can above your head and lost your balance and fell, would you toss the can high enough in the air so that it took a few seconds longer to hit the ground than you did?"

In my mind, I counted out *one … two … three*. A second object would have had to have started its fall somewhat after the first to delay its arrival by three seconds.

"But the maid," I said, "could have misconstrued what she heard, could she not?"

"By a fraction of a second, yes," said Holmes. "By several seconds, not impossible, but highly unlikely. A better explanation is that it was tossed over by someone else after she fell … or was pushed."

We both fell silent until the train approached the station in London, and I ventured one of my own observations.

"Holmes, when we were on the terrace, there were two things I noticed."

"Excellent, and what were they?"

"Well, the surface had been swept clean, but I saw quite a few cigarette butts in the crevasses along the edges where the surface joins the wall."

"An astute observation, Watson. And what else?"

"In three places, there were dark red stains. Not large. But I thought they looked like wine stains. You know how the color seeps into a concrete surface and is hard to get out. There were several patches of it."

"Another diligent observation. Well done, my friend."

"Do you think they are significant?"

"It is much too early to tell."

Chapter Five

The Butcher's Family

The Westbury family lived in a three-story terrace home not far from the Chelsea Common. The neighborhood was one of those that is not particularly rich but still far from poor. I felt a wave of patriotism when I looked at it, remembering that the owner had arrived penniless in London from the Borders, started his career as a butcher's apprentice and retired with a fine home and a chain of shops.

My mood changed to somber upon entering the house. The funeral for Miss Isabella Cecily Westbury had taken place only a few days ago, and the home was overflowing with displays of flowers that had been sent in tribute. An easel beside the staircase held a fine portrait of the young woman. She had been posed standing under an elm tree, holding a book in her arm and gazing into the horizon. Far in the background was a cluster of red-brick buildings, which, upon closer scrutiny, I recognized as Newnham College at Cambridge.

"Did she attend Cambridge?" I whispered to Holmes as we waited for the family to appear.

"Yes. She completed her tripos in mathematics."

"Must have been a clever girl."

"A beautiful face, Watson, does not preclude a brilliant mind."

I was about to make an indignant reply but was precluded myself by the entry of Miss Violet Westbury, and her mother.

"Good morning Mr. Holmes, Dr. Watson," said Mrs. Westbury. "I hope you will excuse the flowers. I left them in place after the funeral. They will fade all too soon, but we are enjoying them as long as we can."

"And so you should, madam," said Holmes.

The mother of Misses Isabella and Violet Westbury was a tall, refined-looking woman of a certain age. Her black attire accentuated her silver hair, and her face, now gaunt, weary, and devoid of any cosmetics, was still undeniably attractive.

She led us into the parlor, where an elderly gentleman stood to greet us.

"This is my father," she said. "Mr. Harris Paterson."

We exchanged greetings as a maid appeared, bearing a tray of tea, coffee, and pieces of fresh fruit.

I could not help but comment on the impressive portrait of Isabella in the lobby.

"Why, thank you, Doctor," said Mrs. Westbury. "Yes, her grandfather arranged for that to be done. He was frightfully proud of her, as we all were. We have one of Violet as well, also from Newnham, but, thank God, she is still with us, and so it resides in the library."

"Sir," I said, turning to the grandfather, "your granddaughter was a lovely young woman. The portrait is brilliant. Please accept my deepest condolences on your loss."

"Thank you, Doctor," said the old man. "We are hoping that Mr. Sherlock Holmes can shed some light on what happened to her."

"Your family, sir," said Holmes, "has endured a terrible loss. Your other granddaughter, Miss Violet, to her credit, overcame her great sorrow and came to me and requested my services."

The old gentleman smiled at the young woman. "Mr. Holmes, do not mistake Violet's youth and petite aspect for timidity. She has a soul of steel."

"She must have to be able to endure tragedies that have already afflicted her. I have agreed to accept this case and give you my word that I shall work diligently toward a resolution. To do so, please permit me to ask some necessary questions, although I warn you that doing so may be difficult and painful to all of you."

"Proceed," said the grandfather. "Whatever happens now cannot be more painful than the news of her death and the funeral. We might not get through it without a few more tears, but they will arrive anyway, so they may as well be in front of you as anybody else."

"Thank you, sir. Permit me to begin with the particulars of your family. Mrs. Westbury, your two daughters were only six months apart in age, were they not?"

"Oh, yes, well, like so many families today, we made a few adjustments. My first husband contracted cancer and died after a long illness. Before he died, he left me with the gift of a baby girl who he did not live long enough to see. He died a week before Isabella was born. For two years, I was on my own. Thank God for my father. He made sure we were taken care of."

"Well done, sir," I interjected. "My profound respect."

The old chap nodded and mumbled something, and the mother continued.

"I had expected," she said, "that my life would continue as a widow with a daughter to raise on my own, but Providence was gracious, and two years later, Dylan Westbury came into my life. His wife had died in childbirth, and we decided, for what were then reasons of practicality rather than passion, to get married. His toddler daughter, Violet, and my Isabella were close in age, and, to our great happiness, we became one loving family. Jack died three years ago. He lived to see his two daughters admitted to Cambridge but passed away before their graduations. We like to believe that he was looking down over the parapets of heaven and as proud as punch."

"I am sure he is," said Holmes, "and not without reason. But now I must ask you about what happened to Miss Isabella, and please, be absolutely frank with me."

"Aye, we can do that," said the grandfather.

"Did she at any time convey to you that she had suspicions concerning the financial management of the Society?"

"About the money?" said Mrs. Westbury. "No, she never said anything to us about the money. She was not comfortable with the living arrangements made for the boys and the girls in the small choir."

"I was informed that they resided in a home for children here in London," said Holmes. "Is that not correct?"

"Not entirely. Izzy said that they all stayed in a private club in St. James Square."

"Which club?" asked Holmes. "East India? Naval?"

"No. It did not have a name. It was a large old house. Members only, but all the members were men. My daughter was not allowed to enter."

"But the children were."

"Yes, and she did not consider that to be appropriate. She had asked about their having access to nurses and school teachers and was assured that some very fine men were looking after those functions."

"Interesting," said Holmes. "But nothing about the finances. You are sure of that?"

"Quite sure." The mother looked at her father and Miss Violet, who nodded their heads in agreement.

"That is good to know," said Holmes. "Now, forgive me, but I must ask a rather personal question."

"Go right ahead," said Mrs. Westbury. "When it comes to the death of my daughter, we have nothing to hide."

"This does not concern her death. It concerns her birth. Was Miss Isabella aware that Lord Bedford Dalgingham was her father?"

A moment of stunned silence was followed by a gasp from Miss Violet.

"Mr. Holmes!" cried Miss Violet. "How dare you!? If you are going to come into our home and insult my mother, then you can leave this minute."

"Before I leave, would you mind terribly answering my question, Mrs. Westbury?"

I was bewildered by what had just taken place in front of me. More bewildering yet was the complete lack of outrage by either Mrs. Westbury or Mr. Paterson, her elderly father.

"Mrs. Westbury?" said Holmes. "Will you answer my question."

"No."

Holmes looked directly at Mrs. Westbury.

"Are you refusing to answer my question? Or did you just do so?"

"I did. Isabella did not know."

Her disclosure was followed by another silence and then another horrified gasp from Violet.

"Mother!" Then Miss Violet looked up at her grandfather, who had said nothing. The anguish in her voice was pitiable.

"Grandfather, you knew. How could you?"

The elderly gentleman stood, slowly walked over to the window, and then turned back to his granddaughter.

"Violet, my dear, please listen and try to understand. I cannot even begin to explain the sadness and heartbreak your grandmother, and I endured as we watched our daughter live in fear, and tears, and agony as she sat by the bed of her loving young husband every evening whilst he slowly died. Dylan had only a few months left to live. The cancer had entered his brain. He had lost his sight and was delirious most of the time. So, when a rich toff came into our office one day to place a large order and started to flirt with your mother, my reaction was, 'why not?' She had already been grieving his loss for over a year. It was only a matter of time before she would be a widow. And here was a wealthy lothario who offered to take her to dinner and the theatre and a trip to Paris. To hear her laugh again made me forget all the social opprobrium that would be unloaded on her if anybody knew. So, yes, my dear, I knew."

"I did not expect," said Mrs. Westbury, "to have a baby as an everlasting reminder of those days. But your sister was born six months after Dylan died. I considered myself blessed by heaven beyond all I could ask or imagine. And then when you and your father came into my life two years later, it was as if the Almighty was telling me that my sins, such as they might have been, were forgiven, and I had been given the gift of a second chance to be loved by a husband and mother to two beautiful daughters."

Miss Violet, with tears streaming down her face, was about to say something, stammered, stood, and walked out of the room.

Holmes paused for a minute and then returned to his questions. He was halted by Mr. Paterson.

"Just wait, Mr. Holmes. She will return presently. Violet is not a shrinking violet."

As he had predicted, Violet Westbury returned to the parlor, sat down, and spoke directly to Holmes.

"Continue with your questions, please, Mr. Holmes."

I detected a glint of admiration in the eye of Sherlock Holmes. He turned again to the mother and grandfather.

"Did Lord Dalgingham acknowledge his patrimony?"

"Oh yes," said the mother, "very generously, and he never stopped, not even after we legally adopted her. Indeed, he paid for the costs of our doing so. He would drop by my father's office regularly and inquire about Isabella's progress. He loved and adored her, howbeit at a circumspect distance. He was very proud of her. His own son, Peter, was already ten years old, and he, quite frankly, did not like him much. When she was in her mid-teen years, he let me know of the need for volunteer helpers at Dr. Barnardo's, where he made it a point of getting to speak with her directly. It was a serviceable arrangement for all of us."

"But Isabella never knew?" said Holmes.

"Never suspected a thing."

"Did his son know?"

"Possibly. The monthly stipends ceased after Lord Bedford, the father, died. But by then, both of my daughters had graduated from Cambridge and were more than prepared to take care of themselves."

Holmes stood and looked again at Miss Violet.

"My sincere apologies, Miss Westbury, for upsetting you. Please understand that this data is highly pertinent to my investigation of your sister's death."

"I do understand. This has been a shock to me. I had not expected it when I asked for your help, but please carry on."

We were on our way out of the house when the old gentleman called to us.

"Mr. Holmes, a question, please."

"Yes, Mr. Paterson, what is it?

"Violet is convinced that her sister's death was not an accident. Do you believe that my granddaughter was murdered?"

"Sir, there is far too little data available to me to make an argument that would stand up in court. I—,"

"Mr. Holmes, I did not ask you if you had a case ready for court. I asked if you believed my granddaughter was murdered."

Holmes paused before answering.

"I have what I can only call my early suspicions. I have learned the hard way not to form a belief. Not yet. Good day, Sir."

Once inside a cab and on our way back to 221B, I demanded an explanation.

"How in the name of all that's holy did you guess that Isabella was Lord Dalgingham's daughter."

"Did you not look at the portraits of Bedford Dalgingham? Did you not observe the painting of Miss Isabella when we entered the house? The family resemblance could not have been more obvious. Immediately, the interest of His Lordship in Miss Isabella all made sense. He was not a foolish old man with a silly attraction to a beautiful young woman. He was a doting father, howbeit somewhat unusually connected to his daughter."

"Right. So, what next?"

"Return to Sussex tomorrow morning."

"To the Five Smooth Stones again?"

"No, Watson. To the solicitor handling the will and the division of the inheritance."

Chapter Six
Where There is a Will

"Is it possible," I asked Holmes as we sat in the cabin of the early train to Sussex, "that whatever happened to Miss Isabella may have had something to do with the estate and not the charity at all? There is a very considerable value to the estate, is there not?"

"I would estimate," said Holmes, "several hundred thousand pounds, counting the various properties and securities. With the English gentry, where inheritances are concerned, anything is possible."

From the Leatherhead Station, it was a ten-minute walk into the center of the town and the law offices of Ditchit, Fast and Hyde. Mr. Harry Hyde, the solicitor for the Dalgingham estate, welcomed us to his office.

"I heard that you came to Linden Hill," he said, "and I was quite disappointed that I did not have an opportunity to meet the famous detective, Mr. Sherlock Holmes, whilst you were here. I am delighted that you found a reason to return. How may I be of assistance to you?"

"I have been asked to investigate the death of Miss Isabella Westbury," said Holmes.

"Yes, I am aware of that. Lord Peter told me that he had hired you to do so. He is very conscientious when it comes to keeping the good name of the Society free from any dark clouds. I assured him that should you call on me, I would give you the utmost cooperation. And now, here you are. How may I help?"

"I have questions concerning the will of Lord Dalgingham and the allocations of the inheritances."

"The will was read shortly after his death. It is a matter now of public record. What do you want to know?"

"Was his daughter the beneficiary of any of his assets?"

"You mean Miss Isabella Westbury?"

"You were aware that he was her father?"

"Yes. It is a foolish man who conceals such matters from his lawyer. I was responsible for looking after the trust His Lordship set up for her when she was born."

"And was any portion of the estate left to her?'

"None."

"Considering his fatherly interest in her, that seems strange, does it not?"

"Not if you're Lord Bedford Dalgingham."

"Sir?"

"Miss Isabella was the oldest. He had four other children in addition to his legitimate son, Peter. There is a set of twins in Montreal, a daughter in Marseilles, and another son in Edinburgh. The youngest has just turned five. He set up trusts for every one of them to see that they were supported until they completed their university studies. Linden Hill was left to Peter. It has been in the Dalgingham family for three hundred years. He was not about to jeopardize that tradition."

"Is Peter aware of his brothers and sisters?"

"He is."

"Are they aware of each other or of the identity of their father?"

"If their mothers have told them, they know the identity of their father. None are aware of each other."

"And what, if you do not mind my asking, is your estimate of the value of the estate that will pass to Peter Dalgingham?"

"Much less than you might have expected, Mr. Holmes. His Lordship had some rather expensive habits—the fathering of offspring being only one. The properties are heavily mortgaged. The net value being handed down to his son is less than twenty thousand pounds. The income from the rents now barely covers the cost of operating the estate."

On arriving back in London, I purchased a newspaper and began to read it whilst we took a cab back to 221B. This notice filled the entire fifth page.

The Times
Final Edition, Friday, 25 September 1896

Help Her Now or Watch Her Die

A Soul-stirring Concert at the Royal Albert Will Melt the Hearts of Londoners and Move Them to Save the Lives of Girls on the Streets of Calcutta

Let us introduce you to Anamika Banerjee, a beautiful, dark-eyed girl of the tender age of thirteen. Her loving mother died when Anamika was only eleven, leaving her as the sole support of her younger brother and sister. The three of them lived in a shack not far from the banks of the mighty Hooghly River. At midnight, a fortnight ago, she ran in panic towards the arms of a police officer, screaming in terror. "Save me! Save me! They are trying to take me!" The constable bravely sheltered the poor waif and raised his nightstick as two mysterious figures faded away into the darkness.

We do not have to tell you, dear Christian citizen of England, what the horrible fate of Anamika would have been. Death? No. A fate worse than death! Years of unspeakable, immoral slavery and then discarded on the miserable wrecks of humanity. That is what would have happened had it not been for the Society for the Care of Street Orphans and our affiliated homes for destitute boys and girls. The policeman took her to the Jewels for Jesus Mission, where she and her siblings now receive nutritious food, clean clothing, and medical attention.

And more than that, the most important of all, Anamika and her little brother and sister now have HOPE!

Do you care enough about the life of a vulnerable girl on the streets of Calcutta to attend a thrilling free concert that will change her life for the better?

This Thursday evening, you are invited to the first in a series of the Isabella Westbury Concerts for the Anamikas of Calcutta. The doors of the Royal Albert Hall will open at seven o'clock, and all are welcome. The Society's brilliantly talented Chorale of Angels will be performing a medley of popular songs and hymns. Your heart will be moved as you listen to the thrilling testimonies of children who once lived on the streets of Calcutta in conditions that are beyond the belief to those of us lucky enough to have been born in the capital city of the British Empire. You will learn how YOU can change the life of one of these poor children. You will learn how YOU can save a child not only from an early death but how YOU can save a tender, vulnerable young girl from a FATE WORSE THAN DEATH.

And best of all, this splendid concert is FREE. All you will be asked to do is to complete and sign a pledge card, promising that every month you will send what you can afford to the Isabella Westbury Fund for Vulnerable Girls. In keeping with the Biblical injunction — *from each according to his ability, to each according to his needs* — those of you whom God has blessed with material wealth are invited to pledge a pound, or two pounds, or ten pounds a month; those of more modest means can send a few shillings.

This special new fund for girls has been established by the Society in honor of the life of Miss Isabella Westbury, a dedicated member of the Directors of the Society whose young life tragically came to an end in a horrible accident. Isabella cared so deeply for the well-being of girls whose lives and virtue are at risk, and in remembrance of her, the President of the Society, Lord Peter Dalgingham, and the General Secretary, Mr. Timothy Olleitch have decided to do something very special that will carry on her work.

"After much prayer," said Mr. Olleitch, "God gave us a vision for a special fund in Isabella Westbury's name, that would allow the Christian people of England to take a direct, personal role in saving the lives of the girls that our beloved Isabella cared about so passionately. We are praying that there will be an abundant response to the start of this appeal and that thousands will subscribe and do whatever they can each month to make a difference in the lives of these poor girls, and to give them HOPE."

MR. SHERLOCK HOLMES HAS BEEN INVITED TO ATTEND. A special guest of the Society, the famous detective, Mr. Sherlock Holmes, has been invited to attend, and a seat has been reserved for him in the front row of the Royal Albert. After the devastating news of the death of Miss Isabella Westbury, the Directors requested that Mr. Holmes conduct a thorough investigation into the circumstances surrounding her passing so that such a terrible tragedy will never happen again.

SET THE DATE NOW ON YOUR CALENDAR. THIS THURSDAY EVENING, COME TO THE ROYAL ALBERT, HEAR THE MARVELLOUS CHORALE OF ANGELS AND TAKE ACTION TO SAVE THE LIVES OF THE ORPHANED GIRLS OF THE STREETS OF CALCUTTA!

"Are you going to attend?" I asked Holmes.

"I would not dream of missing it. It is a splendidly efficient way of gathering every suspect in one place."

The cab stopped in front of 221B Baker, and I prepared to step out, but Holmes grabbed my arm.

"We have been followed," he said. "The cab that stopped a half-block behind us has been trailing us since Victoria."

"Shall we go and accost them?" I asked.

"No. We shall enter our house, immediately exit the postern door, and fetch a cab a block away. The hunted are about to become the hunters. Come now, we have to move quickly."

Chapter Seven

The House on St. James Square

I paid the driver, and we walked casually through the front door and then hustled straight away out the back, through the yard, and into the alley. Three minutes later, we reappeared on Baker Street, a block behind the cab that had followed us and was now sitting parked a few yards from our home.

Taking care not to be seen, we hailed another cab, and Holmes spoke quietly to the driver.

"Sir, we are in need of your services. My name is Sherlock Holmes, and I would be grateful if you could follow the cab that is parked a block in front of us. Would you mind terribly doing that for us?"

"Oww, Sherlock Holmes, is it? Crikey, here I thought I was having another boring day hacking around London, and Mr. Sherlock Holmes sends me off to follow a suspect. Right. Made my day, Mr. Holmes. Can't wait to get home and tell my sons who I had in my cab. They'll have a million questions. Was it a murderer? Was it a spy? Right, he's pulling away now. Here we go."

He kept our cab well back from the one we were following, and we drove south on Baker Street, across Marylebone and down into Mayfair. When we reached Piccadilly, he turned left and, a few blocks further, went right and proceeded along St. James Square. The cab we were following stopped in front of an impressive house, nestled between the London Library and the East India Club. The passenger got out and entered it. Holmes had his spyglass out and was watching carefully.

"Shall we wait here?" I asked.

"No, I suspect that he is staying there for the night. We can leave."

"Do you think this might be the house Mrs. Westbury referred to?"

"Yes. It is the only one that matches her description on the Square."

"Did you get a good look at him?"

"I did."

"Well?" I asked.

"It was that American fellow, Timothy Olleitch."

"Was it?" I said. "Then what was the house he was entering?"

"I do not know," said Holmes. "Therefore, I shall inquire of the nearest expert."

"Who? I do not see anyone nearby."

"Please, my dear Watson, use your imagination."

With that, he leaned his head out of the cab door and shouted. "Driver. Might we have a word with you?"

"If it means helping Mr. Sherlock Holmes, be right happy to."

The driver stepped down from his perch and came and sat inside the cab with us.

"Have you," asked Holmes, "delivered passengers to this address in the recent past?"

"That I have, Mr. Holmes, and to every club and pub up and down Pall Mall and St. James and King and Ryder. Not that many come here, but I've had a few, and we cabbies chat about all these places and the toffs what belongs to them. What does Mr. Sherlock Holmes want to know about it?"

"Tell me about the members who come to that house, please."

"Well, sir, they're all rich, going by the way they're dressed and the briefcases and such they carry. All about the same age. Not old, not young. All quite respectable. Never had to take away any one of them who had been too far into his cups, if you know what I mean, sir."

"Other than their age, anything unusual about them? Anything that sets them apart from all the others who strut and fret their hour upon Pall Mall?"

"Well, seeing as you ask, Mr. Holmes, we cabbies have talked about these men, and it's only men, of course. No women allowed. Now, the other chaps we drop off and pick up in this neighborhood all being to only one club—Boodle's or Brooks or Whites and the like. But only ever just one. You don't see any going regular like to two or three. Always just one. But these chaps, well, they do not belong just to this club. They all belong to this one, plus one of the other toff clubs. Well, we take them back to and from their second club. Or we take them to their place of business or their homes. All work in fine places and lives in excellent neighborhoods. That's all I can say about them that makes them different. Other than that, a toff is a toff, if you know what I mean."

"I do indeed, sir. And I thank you. You have been very helpful. Do you know anything about this club that the man we were following entered?"

"Not a thing except we cabbies wonder if it's a club at all. No name on the door. No other club is happy if a toff has more than one membership, if you know what I mean, sir."

"I do. Very interesting. And now, would you kindly return us to Baker Street?"

Holmes spent the remainder of the day consulting his now multiple volumes of notes on people and organizations in London. He muttered every time he came across a reference to one of the directors of the Society. Meanwhile, I read and continued to put an account on paper of a case we had completed the previous month.

Over supper, Holmes fed himself with one hand whilst holding papers in the other. Other than the occasional "hmmm" or "ah-ha" he was non-communicative.

It had gone eight o'clock when we were disturbed by the bell on Baker Street. Mrs. Hudson appeared a minute later, bearing a calling card.

"He's a bit of a rich gent to be calling this time of the evening, Mr. Holmes," she said, "Fine looking older chap. Must not want to be seen calling on you. My guess is that it has something to do with his wife."

The card she handed us was of the highest quality card stock, with perfectly embossed printing. It announced the visit of a Mr. Marvin Bethune, Senior Partner with Freshmeadows and Gilliams.

Extremely expensive lawyers from select law firms did not make house calls in the evening, and Holmes and I immediately stood to welcome our visitor.

Not waiting for Mrs. Hudson to call him up, Mr. Marvin Bethune climbed our stairs and entered the room. He was dressed in the finest attire available on Saville Row and carried a more casual overcoat over his arm. His full head of silver hair betrayed his age but, although he was no longer young, he had ascended our stairs quickly and exuded a sense of energy and confidence that came, I suspected, with many years of winning legal battles.

We welcomed him, and I asked him if he would enjoy a drink.

"I would, Doctor," he said. "Might you, by any chance, have a bottle of Talisker? If not, then any brand of the water of life would be just the thing for an old fellow."

We did have a bottle of that single malt hidden in the back of the cabinet, and I poured a generous serving. He held it up to the light, smiled, took a slow sip, and smacked his lips.

"My apologies for coming at this uncivilized hour, gentlemen, but I was delayed through the afternoon with another matter than I could not leave."

"Would that," said Holmes, "happen to have been the Rangers game up at Wembley?"

Mr. Bethune looked surprised for a second and then roared with laughter.

"Auch, I had heard you were quite the clever laddie, and so you are. Guilty as charged, Mr. Holmes, and forgive me if I am compelled to cross-question you, but how did you know that?"

"Your accent, sir, has been refined by your university days in Edinburgh, but the remnants of a Glaswegian brogue are still there. Your clothes are of the finest quality, except for your overcoat. You left your good top-coat at your office knowing that you were about to enter the madding crowds and be bumped and jostled by the great unwashed of Scots living in London who will stop whatever they are doing when the Rangers come to town. You will have to send your coat to the cleaners as it is now festooned with spots of dripped beer and grease from a meat pie you consumed whilst occasionally leaping to your feet to cheer on your boys from home."

"I am undone!" he said between bouts of laughter. "Off to prison I go with a panic in my breastie. You have me, Mr. Holmes."

"That, I doubt. However, what I do not know and cannot discern at all is why you have come to call. Now I am at your mercy."

"Are you now, laddie? Well, I read in *The Times* that you had become involved in the affairs of this Society for the Care of Street Orphans."

"Yes, I am somewhat."

"Aye, well, a client of mine, a dear old lady, is deeply concerned about this charity."

"An old lady? Why? Was she swindled by them? Coerced into making a donation she could not afford?"

"Oh, no, she can afford whatever sum you can imagine. This dear old lady lives on Threadneedle Street."

"Oh my," I gasped. "The Bank of England."

"Yes, Doctor. That old lady. Our firm has provided her with legal counsel for over a century. She comes to us whenever she has a problem."

"And you are assigned to take her cases?" asked Holmes.

"Well, no, not normally. I retired from full-time practice a few years ago, but they still call me in when there is something that seems peculiar and of a sensitive nature."

"I am all attention," said Holmes. "Please, Mr. Bethune, enlighten me."

"As you likely know, Mr. Holmes, the Bank serves as the transfer facility when smaller banks wish to send large payments to overseas recipients. Hundreds of these take place every day, and funds are wired all over the world. A small army of dedicated, bonded clerks fill out the forms and send off the telegrams, and most days are exceedingly boring for them, I imagine. But they are charged with reporting on any transactions that they deem suspicious."

"Including," said Holmes, "any made by philanthropic societies that they suspect might not be for charitable purposes?"

"Yes, those are included. Two months ago, one of those diligent clerks came to his supervisor with a concern about this Society for the Care of Street Orphans. It seems that some very large sums of money were being used to purchase securities instead of being used immediately for charitable purposes."

"I am not a lawyer," said Holmes, "but I do not believe that such an action is against the law as long as it only involves a portion of the assets and is justified as setting aside funds for future use."

"Right you are there. And prudent charities know that donors are fickle and that one week people will send funds to the victims of a hurricane in Jamaica, and the next to the construction of a new hospital in Chelsea, and next to the blind, and after that to elderly racehorses and so on and so forth. Aye, wise trustees have known for years that they must set aside funds to carry them through the seven years of lean that follow seven years of plenty. And it appeared that this was indeed what the Society was doing."

"But that was not all, or you would not be here."

He chuckled again and took another slow sip of his Scotch.

"Right you are, laddie. But prudent trustees know that they must not put all their eggs in one basket. Well now, a few months back, a conscientious clerk beavering away in the bowels of Threadneedle Street thought it a bit odd that a charity claiming to help children in India was sending large drafts of money not only off to India but also to Mexico, Bolivia, Poland, Turkey, Peru, and Canada."

"Would that not constitute cautious geographical diversity?" asked Holmes.

"It would if it were not for the fact that all of the funds sent to those countries were transferred to mining companies, specifically companies that specialized in mining silver."

Holmes took out his pipe, lit it, and puffed slowly.

"That is curious," he said.

"I rather think so as well, Mr. Holmes. It is one thing to set aside for a rainy day but another altogether to engage in highly risky speculation with money entrusted to a charity."

"Speculation, Mr. Bethune?"

"Aye. Have you no been following the press about the election in America?"

"Not if I can avoid it."

"They are waging war over the bimetallic question. The candidate for the Democrat and Populist Parties, that William Jennings Bryan fellow, is promising to take the Americans away from sole *de facto* dependence on the gold standard and add silver as a second foundation. Should he win the election in November, the demand for silver will go through the roof."

"And the value," said Holmes, "of shares in those mining companies will do the same."

"Now, Mr. Holmes, does that not strike you as a bit beyond strange?"

"I am not a lawyer, sir, but it would seem to me that it is irresponsible and possibly an abrogation of fiduciary responsibility. The Charities Commissioner might have something to say about it, but it hardly constitutes a major crime. If they are successful, will they not be hailed as uncannily astute directors who reaped a windfall for the poor children of Calcutta?"

'Quite so, Sir. But kindly allow me to pass along a nugget of wisdom from my career as a solicitor. We employ what we call the smell test. If a matter has a whiff of malfeasance, even if there is no immediate evidence, our intuition, our feelings, if you insist, almost always serve as a reliable guide. Barristers are seldom lied to, as there are serious consequences for perjury in a court of law. But we solicitors hardly see a day go by without someone lying to us. And Mr. Holmes, my intuition tells me that someone in this matter is lying."

"Directors who are less than truthful are a dime a dozen. But what is it you wish me to do about it?"

"I wish, Mr. Holmes, to have you agree to contract your services to Freshmeadows and Gilliams and to conduct a thorough investigation of this matter. I further expect that such an arrangement will be utterly and completely confidential. It will be known only to those in this room and to the chap who governs a certain old lady. And I expect you to complete your work and submit a full report to me within three weeks."

I could see that Holmes was struggling not to smile. His accurate, if exalted, opinion of his unique talents made it impossible for him not to be chuffed at the prospect of working for the Bank of England.

"I will accept your commission, sir, with two assumptions on my part. One, that I will have unrestricted access to records of pertinent financial transactions. And two, that your law firm has an office in Calcutta, and that I will receive cooperative assistance from it."

"You have both. There's a very bright young fellow in our Calcutta office, a national by the name of Harish Sundaram. I will let him know that Sherlock Holmes will be in touch with him. And you know how those Indian chaps are. He will be tickled pink."

Chapter Eight

On a Cross of Gold

Two days later, a lengthy telegram was delivered to Sherlock Holmes, having been sent from the Western Union office in Calcutta. It ran:

To: The esteemed Mr. Sherlock Holmes of the very famous address of 221B Baker Street.

From: Mr. Harish Sundaram, Third Chief Assistant Auditor, reporting to the Second Chief Assistant Auditor of the pleasant office of Freshmeadows and Gilliams in Alberta House adjacent to Writers on Binoy Badal Dinesh, Calcutta, West Bengal.

Dear Mr. Sherlock Holmes, Esquire. I was so very very happy myself when I am receiving the telegram from the very respected Mr. Marvin Bethune KC of our headquarters for the whole world in London. I cannot believe my good fortune when I am told I am to have the very big honor of assisting the famous Mr. Sherlock

Holmes. It is a great pleasure to me to have this very big honor.

As a foreign-returned from England, I am doing my graduation very very soon for my certification to be an Accountant with a special talent for Auditing. I belong to Visakhapatnam, but now I live in Calcutta. I am working very very hard and do a lot of auditing of foreign monies that come and go throughout the glorious British Empire.

I am starting on this wonderful new assignment straight away and will pay visits to all of the orphanages whose names Mr. Bethune KC has sent me to verify that they are the recipients of the transfers sent to them through the Bank of England.

I will work most diligently and will have my report ready to send to you within a fortnight. If God is willing, I shall send it sooner.

May fortune continue to smile upon you, Mr. Holmes.

I remain, yours very truly,
Harish Sundaram

"Well, Holmes," I said, "it appears that you have an eager accomplice in Calcutta."

"And several more here in London."

"Here? Who?"

"I have assigned my Baker Street Irregulars to conduct surveillance around the clock on that house in St. James Square."

"You have decided then that the house cannot be ignored? Why?"

"Because this came from the Diogenes Club."

He handed me a note that was written on a rather expensive piece of notepaper in a rather sloppy hand. It ran:

```
Sherlock: I see in the Press that you have
your fingers in the Orphan Street Children
charity. You will keep me informed of anything
and everything you uncover. Come and see me at
six o'clock today at my club. Mycroft.
```

"Oh, my," I said I. "It looks like you have opened a can of worms."

"Or possibly disturbed a hornets' nest. And I find myself in the peculiar position of having four clients who have all conscripted me to work on the same case."

It being a pleasant October day, we departed from Baker Street not long after five and walked down through Marylebone and Mayfair to Pall Mall. We had arrived at the St. James end and turned until we reached a now-familiar door a little way past the Carlton. The porter greeted us in silence and led us to the Stranger's Room. Holmes left me there whilst he went and fetched his older and much stouter brother.

Whilst waiting, a steward of the club arrived bearing a small silver tray with a snifter of brandy.

"This is for Mr. Holmes," he told me. "Would you and the other gentleman who you arrived with like one as well."

"Yes, we would. And you may place it on the account of Sir Mycroft Holmes," I told him, struggling to hide a puerile grin.

Sherlock Holmes returned with his brother in tow. Mycroft Holmes nodded and grunted at me, and deposited his large frame into one of the comfortable chairs. For over a minute, he said nothing as he sat perfectly still, gazing out through the window to Pall Mall. Then he leaned forward and appeared to have fixed his eyes on a man who was walking west on Pall Mall toward St. James Street.

"Look," he said. "There goes one of them now."

"One of whom?" asked Holmes.

"One of those rascals," said Mycroft, "who belong to that curious house up on St. James Square. Name's Fitz Leigh. Son of the baron. He'll be on his way to Brook's. There's about twenty of them who belong in that house."

"Do they own it?"

"It's leased from Westminster by an American firm registered in the State of Delaware. So, no telling who the individual shareholders are. But we have had our eye on it since the start of the year."

"And would you, my dear brother, mind telling me why?"

"Two reasons."

"And in order, they would be?"

"The previous lessee was a fellow by the name of Hugo Oberstein. You sent him off to prison for fifteen years," said Mycroft.

"As he has not escaped, shall we move on to the second reason."

"Because the cowboys who run Washington asked us to."

"By that, I take it you mean they told you to."

"Fine, if you must, Sherlock. Yes, and in no uncertain terms."

"And are you going to tell me why?"

"Because," said Mycroft, now attending to his brandy, "the Americans are obsessed with not letting foreigners tamper with their elections by seducing the public with advertising and trinkets and other forms of legal bribery. They want to keep those tactics exclusively for use by themselves. They have tracked some small amounts of money used to support the Democratic Presidential candidate to that Delaware company and then back to London. If the Democrat wins, there will be no end of accusations that it was British money that put him in power. Now that, of course, is utter rubbish and nonsense, but the Americans are our best friends, whether we like them or not. So, Her Majesty is obligated to investigate those chaps and find out what they are up to. When I saw that you had your nose into them already, I sent a note off to the Cabinet telling them that Mr. Sherlock Holmes would be more than happy to conduct such an investigation."

"And let me guess. You assured them that I would do so *gratis*."

"Yes, of course, I did. You do not need the money anymore after your soaking of Holdernesse. You will offer your services above and beyond the call of duty, just as I do. And you will keep everything you do entirely confidential."

"And are you going to impart to me what you have already learned about them."

"There's a file beside you that has some biographical details on all of the members. What we need you to find out is why, in heaven's name, bluebloods like that lot are trying to elect a Democrat. Have they lost their minds?"

"Not at all, Mycroft. I can tell you why, if you care to ask."

"Then tell me."

"Because they are using the funds donated to the charity to purchase shares in the world's major silver mining companies."

"Ah … the bimetallic question?" said Mycroft.

"Precisely. The Americans may not like their political activities, but there is nothing illegal on this side of the pond about what they are doing."

"Quite the clever lot. So, knowing what you do, have you ceased your investigation of them?"

"Not at all. I suspect that their nefarious activities have led them to do much worse."

"Worse than electing an American Democrat? That is hard to imagine."

"Well. Somewhat worse. Murder."

Chapter Nine

An Evening in the Royal Albert

I saw little of Holmes over the next few days. When I came to the breakfast table in the morning, he had already been up and gone. Twice he returned before I went to bed for the night, but he merely smiled, bade me a good night, and vanished into his bedroom. He did, however, leave the file that Mycroft had given him out of the coffee table with a note to me attached, instructing me to 'read this.'

So, I did.

There were eighteen members of the club that chose not to reveal its name to the public. Several of them, the fellows who served as directors of the charity, had attended Harrow. The others were divided amongst Eton, St. Paul's, Clifton, Charterhouse, and Westminster. Those who had attended Oxford and Cambridge had concentrated their studies on *The Greats,* with particular emphasis on *The Modern Greats.* In addition to Charles Darwin, with whom I was familiar, they had written well-received monographs and led debates on a cluster of other academics I had vaguely heard of—Herbert Spencer, Freidrich Nietzche, and Arthur de Gabineau. The one fellow who had attended the Sorbonne in Paris had become something of an expert on Charles Maurras and his philosophy of *nationalisme intégral.* Quite the well-read chaps, the lot of them.

Beyond their common interest, however, in *avant-garde* thought, there was nothing that Holmes had discerned that had brought them together for a beer in a pub, let alone leasing an exclusive clubhouse on St. James Square. They did not even cheer for the same football teams.

Having completed the file on what I was now calling *The St. James Square Boys,* I took note of the other message Holmes had left for me. It ran:

```
Do not forget that we are honored guests
this evening at the event in the Royal
Albert. Please be dressed and ready to
depart by seven.
```

I was dressed and ready to depart by half-six even though Holmes himself had yet to return. At twenty minutes to seven, he came running up the stairs, rushed into his bedroom, and reappeared fifteen minutes later, dressed to the nines.

"Are you ready?" he asked.

"Holmes, please."

"The madding crowd this evening will likely include no end of raucous children. Hence, it will be over at a relatively early hour, and there will be time for us to enjoy a late dinner at Goldini's. It is only a ten-minute walk from the Royal Albert down to the restaurant on Gloucester Road. Shall we go?"

We hailed a cab and rode down through Hyde Park to Kensington. By the time we arrived at the great hall, the line of waiting to enter was a block long. I sighed my frustration, but Holmes was all good cheer.

"Waiting amongst the populace and eavesdropping whilst doing so," he said, "is a highly entertaining way of gathering pertinent data. Come now, Watson. We can take our place like the obedient London sheep we are."

We marched past a score of families with children, and I must say that I was pleased to see that the Society had not given any priority to the rich and shameless. Working men and their families were standing cheek to jowl behind and in front of the wealthy. To my surprise, all classes seemed to be enjoying the evening and were having a good time chatting and laughing together.

Our wait did not last long. A young fellow, splendidly dressed in gleaming white jodhpuri suit came up to us and quietly asked, in an accent that came from the docklands, if we were Holmes and Watson. Upon confirming that we were, he politely requested that we follow him to our reserved seats. As we departed our place in the line, I overheard several fathers triumphantly whispering to their children, "That is Sherlock Holmes and Dr. Watson."

Upon arriving at the grand steps and main entrance of the hall, we were greeted by several more remarkably attractive young men in Jodhpuri and turbans and lovely young women in saris. We followed two of them to the front row of the orchestra section, immediately below the stage where two seats had ribbons tied across them and our names printed in large letters in the place where the gluteus maximus was about to be rested. We, and all of the attendees, were given an envelope that contained both a set of program notes and a form on which we could indicate our promised monthly donation to the Society.

It took until a quarter to eight for all the crowds to enter and be seated. I cranked my neck around to look at the hall and could see that all but the farthest seats in the second balcony were occupied.

"There must be five thousand people here," I said to Holmes.

"Excellent. That many warm bodies should be enough to silence Albert's Echo."

He was referring to the well-known problem of acoustics within the hall that led to its being famous as 'the only music hall in which a musician can hear himself playing twice.' The massive canvas suspended beneath the domed ceiling had not succeeded in eliminating the echo, but a full house of human bodies was known to help.

A small orchestra entered, filled the pit, and tuned up. With so many children present, the house never became altogether silent, but it subsided to a dull murmur when the President of the Board of Directors, Lord Peter Dalgingham, strode on to the stage and announced the evening, making a point to welcome the notable guests.

He began with some minor members of the Royal Family who were seated in the boxes and descended down the list as protocol required, welcoming a handful of aristocrats, admirals and generals, captains of industry, and somewhat famous artists from the theater and music halls.

"And last but by all means not least," he declared, "is England's and indeed the world's most famous detective, Mr. Sherlock Holmes!" The crowd gave a cheer and Holmes half-stood, half-turned around, and gave a half-a-wave to the crowd.

Then, the recently installed electric house lights were dimmed, and the orchestra began to play what was supposed to sound like Indian music. As it did so, a band of children, all dressed in rags, slowly walked onto the stage. Some were holding rice bowls; others were limping. All had heads bowed. They assembled, sixteen of them, in two rows, with the older eight in the back row and the younger ones in front of them. The orchestra played, and the chorale sang what I assumed was a well-known Indian song in what I assumed was either Hindi or Bengali. Whilst doing so, they either held out their rice bowls or placed the palms together and pretended to beg. After a minute of this pantomime, two young men, both English-looking, appeared. One was dressed in clerical vestments and the other in a British military uniform. They passed along the two rows handing out some sort of voucher, and then, in a very impressive sleight-of-hand, the rice bowls were suddenly full and overflowing. The audience loved the magic trick and burst into a loud round of applause.

"That was splendid," I whispered to Holmes as I joined in the applause.

"For pity's sake, stop looking at the rice bowls and look up into the boxes. And try to remember who you see sitting there."

I glanced up to my left and observed only a host of well-dressed Londoners. I shrugged to myself and returned my attention to the stage.

I watched as the clergyman took the hand of the oldest child and led him offstage. The rest of the chorale, except for one boy, linked their hands together and followed him, with the other chap, the one dressed in a business suit, bringing up the end of the line.

The one boy who was still on the stage moved forward until he was at the edge. One more step and he would have fallen into the orchestra pit. He waited until the hall had gone silent and then began to recite Kipling's poem about the East meeting the West. Every word was spoken clearly and was delivered with just the right amount of emotion.

The audience applauded when the final lines were delivered:

But there is neither East nor West, Border, nor Breed nor Birth,
When two strong men stand face to face, tho' they come from the ends of the
earth.

And then the applause multiplied in volume as the Chorale of Angels reappeared on stage, but transformed and dressed in smart school uniforms. They had been rescued from the streets of Calcutta and were now enjoying the God-given blessings of the British Empire. Together they sang a medley of beloved hymns that conveyed the great hope of the missionary enterprise. In excellent four-part harmony, they sang *Rescue the Perishing, From Greenland's Icy Mountains,* and *Onward Christian Soldiers.* Interspersed with the singing, several of the younger boys and girls recited well-known passages of Scripture.

Once that segment was completed, they moved into a short but intricate pattern of marching around and past each other, accompanied by a rousing orchestral rendition of *All Hail the Power of Jesus' Name.* Then they reassembled and, with beaming smiles lighting up their brown faces, they sang a medley of joyful popular songs that were familiar to anyone who had attended an evening lately in a music hall. *Daisy Daisy, My Grandfather's Clock, The Lost Chord,* and a selection of whimsical pieces by Gilbert and Sullivan brought cheers from the audience.

In the midst of the cheers, Holmes leaned his head toward my ear.

"Do you see the chap standing by the wing curtain on the right?"

"Yes? What of him."

"He was walking down Pall Mall when we were in the Diogenes Club."

"So were a score of others."

"Of course, there were, Watson, but he is the only one now standing in the wing. Do try to remember him."

Beckoned by that fellow, the chorale departed from the stage, leaving only one of the older boys who gave his testimony. He likened himself to Oliver Twist, orphaned and recruited into a gang of thieves. He had been destined to a life of crime and prison had it not been for his having been rescued by the loving mercy of one of the homes supported by the Society for Care of Street Orphans. Now, he was in school every day and had decided that God had called him to be a medical missionary.

When he finished his moving account of his life, he stepped off-stage as the other children re-entered to the marching music of *The British Grenadiers*. They had changed their costumes again, and this time were clad in an odd assortment of patterns with royal blue backing and patches of red and white lines that appeared to be entirely random. As the march came to an end, they assembled in their two lines of older and younger children but with their backs to the audience. With a drum roll and a blast from the brass, they turned in unison, and the crowd let out a roar. Once assembled, their costumes formed a complete Union Jack.

For the next twenty minutes, they delivered spirited renditions of *The British Grenadiers, The Bonnie Banks of Loch Lomond, Men of Harlech,* and *Molly Malone.* In between the songs, two more children gave their testimonies while another two recited familiar portions of Blake's *Jerusalem,* and Browning's touching *Home Thoughts from Abroad.* Enthusiastic applause followed each number.

As the orchestra played *When Mothers of Salem,* the children exited the stage, and Mr. Timothy Olleitch entered and stood on the apron. He spoke—attempting to hide his American accent and his voiced tinged with just the right tremble of emotion—of the miracle God had wrought in the lives of each of these precious children and of the hundreds who were now living in loving Christian orphanages in Calcutta. But such miracles were not possible without the generous support from believers in Britain who gave sacrificially to the work.

"Tonight," he told the audience, "you can be a part of a miracle. You can help save the life of one child who is now living on the streets of Calcutta. You and God together can save that child from a life of crime, depravity, sickness and misery. You can give them hope for the future. And this is how you can do that. Please, each of you, take the envelope you were given as you entered the hall …"

The envelopes contained a photograph of an Indian child, a pledge card, and a small pencil. We were instructed to prayerfully fill out the pledge card with the amount God would have us give to the Society each month, add our names, addresses, and signatures, and then put the card back into the envelope and pass them down the rows to the aisle where the ushers would come and collect them.

Having completed this task, Mr. Olleitch thanked those present for their generous support and then made an unexpected request.

"In our schools, the children learn their maths and reading, and, by the time they graduate, they will have read the entire Bible, the plays of Shakespeare, as well as Homer, Virgil, Chaucer, Dickens, and G.A. Henty. But we cannot mislead you. We have to confess that there is one set of spellbinding stories that they love above all else. I am referring, of course, to the splendid accounts by Dr. Watson of the adventures of Sherlock Holmes."

That brought a laugh and applause from the crowd. Mr. Olleitch continued.

"When we told our Chorale of Angels that Sherlock Holmes would be present tonight, they asked me to make a special request. They wanted to know if, on Saturday, when they do not have classes, Sherlock Holmes himself would take them on a guided walk through London, stopping at all those places where crimes had taken place and criminals apprehended. Now, we had to pray before granting that request because, as you know, some of the stories are perhaps not the most morally uplifting. But we agreed that these children, these angels, these miracles of God's grace, deserved such a treat. And so, on their behalf, I am asking Mr. Sherlock Holmes if he could make himself available to the children on Saturday to guide them through London. What do you say, Mr. Holmes? Can they count on you for a well-deserved outing?"

The audience all began to clap in unison and started a unison chant of "Yes, yes, yes."

Holmes waved his hand and nodded several times and received a round of applause.

"And now," announced Mr. Olleitch, "let us welcome back the Chorale of Angels as they bid us good night."

From stage left, the children walked onto the stage, each bearing a small candle and each dressed in either beautiful saris or Jodhpuri suits and turbans. They assembled, and the orchestra struck up a song that had been introduced to London only a year earlier. It was the children's *Evening Prayer* from the opera *Hansel and Gretel*. Since the debut in Daly's Theatre, it had become exceptionally popular, although nobody could believe that the composer's true name was something so absurd as Engelbert Humperdinck.

The smallest girl came forward and thanked the crowd for their love and care and announced that they would always remember the kind and generous people of London. Then, as the house lights were dimmed, the chorale sang a lovely, sweet rendition of *Abide with Me*.

As soon as they had finished, the five thousand people all leapt to their feet and delivered sustained and thunderous applause. One chap shouted, "Encore!" and the crowd took it up.

The tallest boy and the tallest girl came forward and stood at the front of the stage and waited for the audience to become quiet and sit down. The orchestra struck one introductory chord, and the two of them began to sing.

When Britain first, at heaven's command,
Arose from out the azure main,
Arose, arose, arose from out the a-azure main,
This was the charter, the charter of the land,
And guardian angels sang this strain:

The audience began cheering as they sang, and when they reached the chorus, the boy stretched out his arms, palms up, and gestured to the crowd to stand. In response to his shout of "Join us!" we all filled the hall with the great words:

RULE BRITANNIA!
BRITANNIA RULE THE WAVES
BRITONS NEVER, NEVER, NEVER SHALL BE SLAVES

On the second verse, the rest of the children joined the duo, and then the audience joined in again on the chorus. Once we reached the end of the song, the children bowed to the roaring approval of the crowd and made their way off the stage. The atmosphere in the Royal Albert Hall was as if charged with electricity. The smiles and laughter of both adults and children were a joy to behold.

"Wasn't that grand!" I shouted to Holmes above the din of the crowd as we shuffled our way toward the exit.

"Utterly brilliant."

"So good of you to agree to taking them on Saturday!"

"Did I have a choice?"

Chapter Ten

A Day with Children Can be Dangerous

Saturday, 25 October, began as an ideal day to take an adorable group of children for a guided tour of criminal London. Holmes and I had planned out a route that would begin at the Nelson Monument and walk south to the Northumberland Hotel. There, where Hugh Baskerville had lost his boot, the boys and girls would be re-told the terrifying story of The Hound. It would not be far from there to Scotland Yard and then over to the East End.

"I thought we might stop in at the Ten Bells Pub," said Holmes.

"The haunt of Jack the Ripper?" I said.

"Precisely."

"Are you trying to paralyze them with fear?"

"Even small spines enjoy being tingled," he said.

We had risen early and enjoyed breakfast together as we made final plans for the day's outing. It was a bright, sunny morning but, being late October, decidedly cool. I had donned my wool twill trousers and a heavy sweater and was all prepared to depart when a knock came to the door. A messenger boy delivered to me an envelope marked with the name and insignia of St. Mary's Hospital. I opened and read it.

"Oh, no," I sighed. "Of all days."

"What is it?" asked Holmes.

"I cannot go with you. I have to go over to the hospital. Lady Chadbrand had a heart attack. She has been my patient for years, and the hospital is requesting my immediate presence to consult with me on her treatment. I am so sorry, Holmes."

"Not to worry, my good man. I shall not be lost without my Boswell. I shall put my remembered acting skills to use and will entertain the children."

"Do try not to leave them having lost their wits."

"I shall do my very best by myself to render them trembling and quaking with fear. What fun would there be for them if it were just another dry, boring historical tour?"

"Holmes, you are incorrigible."

"Thank you. I try."

We departed 221B, and Holmes hailed a cab to Trafalgar Square whilst I hurried on foot the dozen or so blocks over to St. Mary's. Once I arrived there, I inquired straight away concerning Lady Chadbrand. The nurse at the desk informed me that she had been brought in very early this morning complaining of severe pain that was indicative of a heart attack. Now, however, she was sleeping, and the attending physician had directed the staff not to disturb her. He, having been at the end of his night-time shift, had returned to his home to catch up on his sleep and would be back at the hospital by 10:00 am.

"I am so sorry," said the nurse, "to inconvenience you like this, but would mind terribly waiting for Dr. Jeddler to return? He needs to speak to you regarding the further treatment of the patient."

I shrugged in exasperation. There was nothing I could do to change the situation and, so, I went and sat in the visitors' lounge and read stories from the stacks of months-old magazines.

At half-past ten, a young doctor came and found me and, all apologies, thanked me for my patience and promptly excused himself to check on one or two other patients, assuring me that he would return in two shakes of a dead lamb's tail.

He came back a half-hour later, and together we went to the room where Lady Chadbrand had been placed. The dear old lady was sitting up in bed and looking not-at-all like someone who had just suffered a coronary attack. She looked at me as I entered and smiled.

"Oh, Dr. Watson, so good of you to come. Everyone thought I had a heart attack, and, for a while, I thought that was what had happened to me. But my heart is pumping away as regularly as can be. Just don't ask me to move."

"My dear lady," I said, "what happens when you move?"

"Every muscle in my upper body hurts. I really don't know what brought it on. Maybe I have caught some dread disease from the Orient. It came on whilst I was getting ready for bed last night. I was just fine, and then I started to feel a pain in my upper arms, and then it expanded to my shoulder and then across my chest and then my back. Within ten minutes, I could hardly breathe. Fortunately, my nephew was at the house, and I told him that I must be having a heart attack. He, bless him, brought me here straight away where they poked and prodded every corner of me and listened to my heart a dozen times."

"We have," said Dr. Jeddler, "examined her every way we know how. Other than severe pain in her skeletal muscles of her torso, there does not appear to be anything wrong with her."

I examined her quickly, listening to her heart and lungs, and doing my share of poking a prodding. Other than muscular complaints, there was nothing wrong with her.

"What," I asked her, "were you doing yesterday?"

"I am in the midst of making some changes in the house and had to move some things around. My nephew surprised me with a visit and offered to help. He was a godsend. By the end of the day, we had so much done."

"What were you moving?"

"Only furniture and boxes of books. The library is going upstairs. And, oh my, that was quite the spot of work. My dear husband, bless his heart, was somewhat of a hoarder when it came to books. When he died, he left me with two thousand of them, and they completely ruined the look of the parlor. So off they went."

"And how many of them did you move?" I asked.

"Half of them. I did my share. That was only fair. I wasn't going to have my nephew move them all."

"Lady Cradbrand," I said in a firm doctorly manner, "may I remind you that you are—,"

"I am what, Doctor Watson? I am sixty years old and as fit as a fiddle. And I make sure I eat a healthy diet and get vigorous exercise. A day of moving books and a few pieces of furniture is just what a lady my age needs to keep doing to keep her body working."

"Do you not have staff to do that for you?"

"Of course, but they had other responsibilities, and I was not about to hire men to do what I could jolly well do myself. The Lord helps those who help themselves, is what I've always said."

"That He does, madam. He also designed our bodies so that we are protected from continuing to do harm to ourselves. You did not have a heart attack. You are suffering from a chest cavity spasm. It strikes us when we indulge in a long period of strenuous physical work when we have not been accustomed to doing in the past. It is your body's way of saying 'stop.' Now then, what you need to do is go home, take a long, hot bath with Epsom salts, treat yourself to a generous brandy, and rest. In two days, you will be fine again. But from now on, no more than fifty books in one day. And no more moving furniture. Is that understood, Lady Chadbrand?"

The dear old soul smiled sheepishly. "Yes, Doctor. Whatever you say."

"And, Dr. Jeddler," I said, "would you mind sending a copy of your report on this incident over to me? I am currently staying on Baker Street. There is no rush."

"Certainly, Dr. Watson. I'll have it in your hands by this afternoon. You do not have to tell us the address. After Buckingham Palace, it is the best known in London."

I bade the lady and doctor a good day and returned to Baker Street. It was close to the noon hour, and I wondered if there was any possibility of my finding Holmes and the children and joining up with them. But all Holmes had told me of his planned itinerary was that he was headed for the East End. There was no telling which dodgy lane he would now be taking them down. So, I resigned myself to giving that idea a pass and spending the remainder of the afternoon reading the latest novel to arrive from Mudie's. It was a rollicking adventure yarn about the hapless King of Ruritania, and by four in the afternoon, I was thoroughly engrossed in it.

My reverie ended when the bell sounded on Baker Street, and a messenger boy delivered an envelope from St. Mary's. With regret, I laid *The Prisoner of Zenda* aside and read the report on Lady Chadbrand. It may have been dictated by a doctor, but it was legible and, therefore, must have been written by a secretary. The content quickly covered all the salient points of her presentation, diagnosis, tests, and treatments and concluded with a very flattering and generous account of my visit. The patient had been discharged at two-thirty that afternoon and returned to her home in Kensington.

I was about to set the report aside when something on the admission form caught my eye.

Her next of kin was *Peter Dalgingham, nephew.*

The immediate, reasonable conclusion would have been that it was just a coincidence. However, I had spent far too many years with Sherlock Holmes to assume for a second that anything that took place in the criminal world could be coincidental.

Try as I might, I could not return my concentration to the adventures of Rudolph and Flavia, and I had to content myself with a glass of brandy and wait for Holmes to return.

At five o'clock, I heard the door on Baker Street open and Holmes's familiar footfalls climbing the stairs. What was utterly unusual was that he was singing quietly to himself.

He never does that.

He entered the room and was beaming happily.

"Good afternoon, my dear Watson. I am so sorry you could not come with us. I had a thoroughly delightful time with those children. They are splendidly well-mannered, bright, articulate, and have an unhealthy obsession with stories of criminals—the nastier, the better. I have not had such an enjoyable few hours since the day I sent my first murderer off to the gallows. And what about you, my good man? How was your dear old patient with the heart attack?"

As he was pouring himself a glass of sherry, I recounted my examination of Lady Chadbrand and then laid the admissions form in front of him.

"Somehow, Holmes," I said, "I doubt that my being called away to see her was merely a coincidence."

"Of course, it wasn't. As soon as your summons arrived here this morning, I assumed that it was a ruse to get you out of the way and leave me on my own all day with those marvelous children."

"But why would Peter Dalgingham, or anyone for that matter, want to do that?"

"At the moment, I do not know. However, there is no doubt a reason, and we shall discover it in due course. Now then, what do you say to some supper? Shall I let Mrs. Hudson know that we wish to eat at six?"

At the appointed hour, Holmes and I sat down to a fine supper of lentil soup, roast pork loin, and dill loaf. We were preparing ourselves for dessert when a loud series of knocks resounded up the staircase from Baker Street.

"Are you expecting anyone?" I asked, seeing the possibility of dessert and brandy vanish before it had even arrived at the table.

"Not this soon, but I am not surprised."

I stepped down to the front door and opened it. Standing, and looking quite intimidating in their uniforms, were two police constables.

"Are you Mr. Sherlock Holmes?" one of them asked.

"No, I am not."

"This is his address. Do you know where he is?"

"Yes, I do."

"Well then, where is he?"

"He is upstairs taking his supper. If you would return in thirty minutes, he will be available to see you. Good evening, gentlemen," I said as I started to close the door.

They were having none of that.

The two of them pushed past me and barged up the stairs. I scampered up behind them.

"Are you Sherlock Holmes?" they demanded of Sherlock Holmes.

"Indeed, I am. Shall I pour two more cups of tea, gentlemen?"

"Mr. Sherlock Holmes, you are under arrest."

Chapter Eleven

Arrested for What!?

"Oh dear, what have I done now?"

"You are charged with gross indecency in accordance with the Criminal Law Amendment Act."

One of the constables then advised Holmes of his rights and demanded that he follow them to the offices of the Metropolitan Police.

I was horrified. At least I was until he looked back at me with that unmistakable twinkle in his eye.

"Well, don't just stand there, Watson," he said. "Come along."

"No, sir," said the constable. "This is only about you, Mr. Holmes. Companions are not permitted."

"But," said Holmes, "this man is my acting solicitor, and under British Common Law, he is legally entitled to come with me, and you would be in violation of the law to forbid him."

That produced a confused look on the face of the constable.

"Are you," he asked me, "the solicitor for Sherlock Holmes?"

"I am now, indeed," I said and followed them down the stairs and out to the police wagon.

"Holmes," I said once we were locked in the back of the carriage, "please stop being so flippant. This is serious."

"It is indeed. I could end up in Reading Gaol, sharing a cell with Oscar Wilde. I expect he would provide a serious intellectual chatter to challenge my imagination."

"Sometimes, Holmes, you are impossible."

Upon arriving at the offices of Scotland Yard, we were escorted straight away to the basement and put in one of the cells. The constable informed us that whilst I was free to leave anytime, Holmes would have to wait here until an Inspector arrived, who would deal with him.

"And would that be Chief Inspector Lestrade?" Holmes asked.

"It would. He has been sent for," said the constable as he departed.

"Holmes, you must tell me what this is all about!"

"I will. But not now. We have at least a half-hour in which we cannot possibly be disturbed. I will redeem the time with thought and contemplation. May I suggest that you take out your notebook and pencil and jot down all the details of what has recently taken place. Your readers will, I assure you, enjoy the account. Did you remember to note the names of the constables, or the look and smell of the interior of the police wagon, or the sounds we heard as we were being led along the passage toward this cell? Good writers never neglect those details."

In my alarm, I had not noted any of those, and thus they do not appear in my account of the evening.

Whilst I attended to my notes, Holmes closed his eyes, tented his fingers, and disappeared behind his wall of silence. His concentration was abruptly terminated twenty minutes later when the door at the end of the hallway crashed open, and a familiar voice bellowed.

"Sherlock Holmes!" said Inspector Lestrade, "What in the name of all that is holy are you doing in one of my cells?"

"I fear, my dear Inspector, that you shall have to ask one of the two constables behind you as they were the ones that arrested be. Mind you, they conducted themselves entirely by the book, and I commend their deportment."

Lestrade had arrived at the door of our cell and stopped and turned to the police officers who had accompanied him.

"Well, is that true? Were you two the ones who arrested this man?"

"Yes, Inspector, sir. We were."

"And what did you charge him with?"

"Gross indecency, Inspector, sir, under the Labouchere Amendment of the Criminal Law Act."

Lestrade looked stunned. "Holmes? What did you do?"

"It would be more efficient, my dear Inspector, if you were to ask the constable *when* such a felony took place rather than *what.*"

Lestrade turned to the police officers. "Right. So, *when* did this nefarious act take place?"

"Earlier this afternoon, Inspector, sir. This man was with a group of children and behaved in an indecent manner toward two of the girls. They reported it to one of their guardians, and he reported to us."

Now Lestrade appeared momentarily confused before shouting back at the constable.

"Bloody hell! He did nothing of the sort. He was with me and two uniformed policemen from the time he met those children until the time they were returned to their home. Do you think I would not have noticed if he were being a cad? He behaved like a gentleman the entire time."

"You were with him, Inspector, sir?"

"Yes! We met them at Nelson's at nine and dropped them off in St. James Square at four. He and I were together that entire time. Whoever those girls were, they have filed a false report. Now, get out of here and go and find them and bring them here tomorrow morning."

"If I may," said Holmes, "permit me to suggest that you change your charge to the officer, Inspector. The girls, I am sure, are innocent. Whoever amongst their guardians made the report is the more likely culprit."

"Did you hear that?!" said Lestrade to the two constables who were now looking decidedly uncomfortable. "Go and find whoever made the report and bring him in. Open the cell door and release this man. Now. Right. Dismissed."

Lestrade led us to the front entrance of Scotland Yard, muttering to himself as he did so. Then, just before we reached the door, he turned and glared at Holmes.

"You knew you were being set up, didn't you, Holmes! Here I thought you invited me to accompany you on your walk through criminal London with those delightful children out of the goodness of your heart."

"The children," said Holmes, "loved all the stories you had to tell. You have quite the devoted group of fans, Inspector."

"To the blazes with my fans, Holmes. You used me to cover you. You knew this would happen, and you used me."

"It is possible that I might have suspected something."

"Which means that there is something going on behind this society for children. Right, Holmes?"

"A distinct possibility, Inspector."

"Is it now? Well then, out with it. Everything you know or even suspect. You brought me into this case, so it is no longer just yours. Get into my office and start talking."

We flowed Inspector Lestrade to his office. He closed the door and turned and glared at Holmes. "I'm listening, Holmes, and I do not have all night."

As we stood in an office of Scotland Yard, Holmes proceeded to tell the pertinent facts of the case and a few of his not-yet-certain suspicions. Lestrade made notes, and scowled.

Chapter Twelve

Girls in the Night

It was well into the evening by the time we returned to Baker Street. A dense yellow fog had settled down on the streets of London, limiting visibility and rendering the night quite unpleasant. Holmes insisted that we enjoy a late, cold supper. An hour in the familiar room, with a cheerful blaze in the hearth and away from the swirling miasma, was a capital offer.

Dear Mrs. Hudson promptly organized a fine plate of cold meats, breads and fruit, and we nibbled and chatted for an hour or more, followed by another half-an-hour over Port. By then, it was past ten-thirty, and I was weary and anxious to get to my bed. I had just stood and turned toward the stairs to my bedroom when the bell on Baker Street rang. So, I descended the stairs and opened the door.

Standing on the pavement directly in front of me was a senior member of Holmes's Irregulars. He was a somewhat beefy young fellow whose true name I did not know. He had awarded himself the moniker of 'Bulldog,' and it was by the name alone that anyone knew him.

Standing behind him were two young women. It might be more accurate to call them girls as I guessed their age at around fifteen years. Both were dark-skinned and dressed in black saris, with a black scarf covering their heads.

"Good evening, Dr. Watson," said Bulldog. "Is Mr. Holmes in?"

"He is, but it is rather late to be calling on him."

"Aye, it is, sir. But these two young ladies told me they had to speak to him and that I was to bring them to him and so I brought them."

"Very well, then, go on up," I said.

"Follow me," said Bulldog to the girls. "Don't be afraid. He's queer, but he's not dangerous."

As the girls entered and came into the light, I recognized them. They had been members of the Chorale of Angels that Holmes and I had listened to in the Royal Albert Hall.

I decided that perhaps I was not that tired after all, and I followed them upstairs.

"Hello, Bulldog. And hello as well, Miss Yamini and Miss Arunima," I heard Holmes say as the girls entered the room. "Such a pleasant surprise to see you again."

From behind the trio, I watched as the two girls shyly stepped in ahead Bulldog and stood directly in front of Holmes. Both placed their palms together under their chins and bowed ever so slightly.

"Good evening, Mr. Holmes," said the one who Holmes had addressed as Yamini. "Please forgive us for coming so late and without a proper appointment."

"Oh, do not apologize. I am delighted to see you. I enjoyed my time with you and the other children today, and I thank you for coming to see me. However, it is rather late for two girls your age to be out on the streets of London. It is not entirely safe, you know."

"Yes, Mr. Holmes, we know that, but our friend Master Bulldog accompanied us, and he made sure we were kept free from danger."

"Ah, well done there, Bulldog," said Holmes, looking at the stout young fellow who appeared to be thoroughly chuffed with himself.

"However," said Holmes, "there must be a special reason for your coming to see me at this time of night. To what do I owe the honor?"

"Sir," said Miss Arunima, "please forgive us again as the matter is highly indelicate and not at all in keeping with conversations between girls of our age and much older gentlemen. The matter relates to activities that are considered indecent and morally unacceptable."

Holmes merely nodded, but I could see a look of fear spreading over the face of Master Bulldog. He was blushing uncontrollably and appeared to be on the verge of panic.

"Uh, excuse me, Mr. Holmes," he blurted out. "Maybe it would be best if I waited down on Baker Street."

He did not wait for an answer and quickly fled the room, descended the stairs taking several of them at a time, and crashed through the door to the street. Inwardly, I chuckled at the bravery of young English lads who would not hesitate to rush into a ruckus, knowing that they might have their lights punched out, but who turned tail and ran when a conversation turned to those matters that were the rightful private domain only of husbands and wives, or between mothers and daughters on the night before a wedding.

"My dear young ladies," said Holmes, "Let me remind you that I am a detective, and Dr. Warson is a medical doctor. We have been told many indelicate things in complete confidence. It is part of our responsibility to my clients and Dr. Watson's to his patients. So, please, be seated and tell us the complete matter. Do not leave out any detail even if you find it embarrassing to speak of it. No one outside of this room will ever know what you have said."

The two of them, who seemed somewhat ill at ease, sat on the sofa and began by fully introducing themselves.

"My name," began the first, "is Yamini. It means 'child of the night.' My father's name is Mukherjee. My family belongs to Delhi, where my grandparents and my aunties and uncles and most of my cousins are still living, but we moved to Calcutta when my father became an officer in the Indian Army."

"And my name," said the second, "is Arunima. It means 'first light of the morning.'" My family moved to Calcutta from Pondicherry when my father accepted a position as a senior manager in the Writers' Building. My family is much smaller than Yamini's, and I have only two brothers and three sisters, of which I am the youngest."

"Pardon me," I said. "Then neither of you are orphans?"

"Oh, goodness gracious," said Yamini. "No, Doctor. None of us are orphans. All of the members of the Chorale of Angels come from very respected families."

"But ... but on stage, they said you were orphans from the streets of Calcutta."

"Oh, goodness gracious, Doctor. That is the role we play on the stage. We were all selected because we had some talent—that is what we were told. We do not wish to be boastful—for singing and public speaking and dramatic acting. No, no, Doctor. The Society would never put real orphans on a stage in London. It would be a disaster. Those poor children would not have the faintest idea what to do. And once they arrived in England, they would all run away, for being a beggar in England is much better than being a beggar in Calcutta."

"Of course," said Holmes. "Now, your story, please. Do the needful. Be concise but do not leave out any pertinent details, regardless of how indelicate they might be."

"Yes, sir. Indeed, sir. We shall do that," said both of them, more or less in unison. Miss Yamini began.

"After the concert in the Royal Albert Hall, we were all quite excited because the response of the audience was first-class. And we were all thrilled to bits because we performed in honor of Lady Isabella Westbury, of whom we had become very fond. The directors of the Society took us out for treats and sweets and even scones and clotted cream. And when Arunima and I were enjoying our treats, two of the directors came to us and said that they had another surprise for us. Now, you should tell them about that, Arunima."

"Oh, yes," continued the second girl. "Uncle Decimus and Uncle Montague took us aside and said many kind things to us. They said that amongst all of the members of the Chorale of Angels, we were the most diligent scholars and had taken all the best prizes for writing stories. They told us that the *Strand* magazine had announced a contest for scholars from anywhere in the Empire to write a new story and enter it into a competition. And because we were the best scholars and had taken the prizes in our schools for writing, they selected us to write a story."

"And," said Arunima, "it was not just any old story. It had to be about Sherlock Holmes. And we were free to imagine whatever we wanted and turn it into a thrilling mystery story."

"Ah, just like Dr. Watson," said Holmes.

I ignored Holmes's comment. "You don't say," I said. "What a wonderful idea. I hope you were not overly sensational. Mr. Holmes does not like that at all."

"Oh, no, Doctor. At first, we wanted to write a frightening story about murder most foul and intrigue and revenge and stabbings and poisonings and so on. But we decided we had to be sensible. Those were not acceptable topics for girls from good families."

"Well then, if you could not include anything nasty, what sort of mystery could you write?"

"Oh, we did not write a mystery all at. We wrote a romantic story. We told everyone about how Mr. Sherlock Holmes had secretly married Miss Irene Adler and that they had a beautiful cottage in the highlands of Scotland."

Sherlock Holmes grimaced.

Chapter Thirteen

You Will Not Fit

"And just what," said Holmes, "has that to do with you coming at this hour of the night to speak to me?"

He was rather abrupt and, I feared he would upset the girls. But they carried on. Miss Arunima replied.

"Oh, goodness gracious, Mr. Holmes, sir. It has everything to do with it. You see, sir, Uncle Decimus, and Uncle Montague told us that the deadline for submissions was the night before last. The two of us had only a day to write the story, and so we worked very, very diligently until we had finished it and re-written it, and re-written it again until we were happy with it. We were quite sure that you would like it, Mr. Holmes. We made Miss Irene Adler quite ravishing, and you finally fell in love, and the two of you lived happily ever after."

"Get back to your story, please," said Holmes.

"Oh, yes, sir," said Yamini. "Well, sir, we gave the story to Uncle Decimus, and he read it over and told us it was wonderful, and then he gave us the form for making a submission to the contest. We had to sign the last page of the form and swear that we alone had written the story, and that no adult had helped or corrected our work, and that we had taken care not to say anything about any living person that was not true. Of course, that was all fine with us, and we signed the form, and he took the story from us and assured us that he would deliver it straight away to the office of the Strand. But he told us that we were not to talk about it with anyone else because it might make some of the other children in the Chorale jealous and hurt their feelings."

"Yes, of course, and then what happened?" said Holmes.

"One of the boys," said Yamini, "in the Chorale of Angels has the good name of Rajiv. Did you meet him today, Mr. Holmes?"

"Yes. He is the one who is tall and slender and has a thin face."

"Yes, yes, that is he. His father is a barrister and tells him many, many stories about criminals and trials he likes to imagine himself as a detective, and he tells us to call him Sherlock because you are his hero and he looks like you, and he uses words like *singular* and *elementary* and *pray* and *curious* and all those other words that you use all the time. And he keeps on telling us that when you eliminate the impossible—,"

"And what about this Rajiv fellow?" said Holmes.

"Well, sir, we do not wish to get him into trouble, but because he likes to think of himself as a detective, he likes to spy on people all the time and learn their secrets. And he learned how to unlock the door to the office of the Society in the house we are living in, and at night, after midnight, he goes into the office and reads all the files and letters and telegrams that have been received and sent."

"A gentleman," said Holmes, "does not read another gentleman's mail."

"Oh, yes, Mr. Holmes. Rajiv knows that, but he says that detectives only have to be gentlemen in public. In private, they could not truly be gentlemen if they were to be good detectives."

I suppressed a smirk.

"Perhaps," said Holmes, "and what did master Rajiv discover?"

"Last night, he found an envelope that was to be delivered to Scotland Yard. He opened it, and he found the story Arunima and I had written. But it was not our story. The page we had signed swearing that we alone had written the story was there, but the story was entirely different."

"Was it now? And tell me—and do not withhold any detail even if it is embarrassing—the contents of the new story."

It is difficult for me to know if they were blushing, given the darker hue of their faces. However, these two remarkable and articulate young women recounted a litany of indecent offenses made against their persons by none other than Sherlock Holmes. I shall not describe these immoral acts in detail as I do not wish to disturb the moral sensibilities of my readers. Suffice it to say, that they were as appalling as anything I had heard about in my years of medical practice.

"Did Rajiv," asked Holmes, "come and tell you about what he found?"

"Not at first, sir. Like Master Bulldog, he is a boy and was too embarrassed to speak to a girl about what he read. And he found it last night before we had accompanied you during the day today. He thought that we had secretly written a very perverse story and were going to submit it to a magazine like *The Pearl* or *The Oyster* and receive payment. He thought we were very, very clever for doing so. But he could not understand why we would be sending it to Scotland Yard. He thought that maybe some inspector there was going to read it first and mark it as approved. Rajiv is a very nice boy, and we do not want to speak unkindly about him, but we agree that it is a good thing that he has a wealthy father."

"No doubt. However, today he did come and tell you about it."

"Oh, yes, sir. After we spent the entire day with you, even Rajiv was bright enough to see that the story was not true and had been written to falsely accuse Mr. Sherlock Holmes. When he understood that, he overcame his shyness and came and told about what he had read. It was then we knew that we had been tricked and that we had to come and speak to you."

"How did you know that Master Bulldog could help you?"

For the first time, the two of them looked somewhat embarrassed and dropped their gaze downward. Yamini answered.

"Over the past fortnight, we have met all of the Irregulars that you sent to spy on the house."

"Did you now? How did that happen?"

Again, they looked ill at ease, and again Yamini answered.

"At night, sir, after dark, we have been able to escape the house and come out into the street."

"You don't say. How did you do that?"

"There is a small window in the basement level that we can fit through. We met your Irregulars the first night they came to watch the house for you. Every night since then, they have taken us exploring all over London until just before dawn. It has been a wonderful adventure for us, sir. Your Irregulars are very jolly boys even if they are not very good spies."

Holmes paused and thought about that one before giving then a rather stern look.

"Such behavior is highly inappropriate for young women from good families."

"Oh, yes, Mr. Holmes, we know. But please understand, sir. When our tour of England ends, we will return to Calcutta, and within two years, tall and fair husbands from good families will be chosen for us, and we shall spend the rest of our lives as proper Indian wives and mothers. Our time in London is the only opportunity we will ever have for adventure, and we could not let it escape us."

Holmes continued his questions. "Did any adults know about your escapades? Any of the directors of the Society, for instance?"

"Oh, no. We could not tell them. We would have told Lady Isabella, but she was taken from us. During our visits to the Dalgingham estate, we had met her, and she was very kind to us. We told her about our lives and dreams of adventures."

Holmes paused again before posing his final demand.

"Your coming to speak to me was very courageous of you. However, if you are to be truly useful to me, you will now take me and Dr. Watson to the house in St. James Square, show us the window, and allow us to inspect the house so that we can confirm whether or not there are any more pieces of false evidence."

"Oh, no. Sorry, sir. So very sorry, sir. But that is not possible."

"Why not? The two of you and all of the senior members of the Chorale have escaped and returned several times, why could not Dr. Watson and I?"

"Oh, sir, I am not sure how to tell you the answer to that. You might not like what we say."

"Then just blurt it out. Come now, say it."

"Both of you, even you, Mr. Holmes and especially Dr. Watson, are too fat to fit."

In my mind, an image emerged of either Sherlock Holmes or me becoming stuck partway through our descent into a basement window, our arms flailing, and our legs being tugged. I thought it quite comical and chortled to myself. Sherlock Holmes did not show any signs of being similarly amused.

"Very well, then, girls. Thank you for coming to see me. I believe Dr. Watson will be able to show you out and find a cab to take you home."

They followed me out to Baker Street, where a cab eventually emerged out of the fog, and I hailed it. After instructing the driver to take the two of them and Master Bulldog back to St. James, I thought for a minute about sitting down to chat with Holmes. I decided against it and went to bed.

The following evening, another summons, a rather ominous one, arrived from Holmes.

Chapter Fourteen

Mr. Marvin Bethune Returns

It had gone six o'clock in the evening when a bicycle boy knocked on the door of my surgery with a note from Holmes. This one ran:

Please be present at 221B at ten. Dress in dark clothing. Bring service revolver, mask and rucksack. S.H.

At ten o'clock, I was waiting in the front room when Holmes appeared.

"What do you say, Holmes? Ready for a night—,"

I did not finish what I was about to say. Holmes had brought company. Behind him was the distinguished lawyer, Mr. Marvin Bethune.

"Good evening, Dr. Watson," he said as he entered. "So glad that you arrived. Your friend, Mr. Holmes, is offering generous libations of the water of life. I suggest you join in."

His words were friendly, but his countenance was somber.

I mumbled a greeting, and we sat down. I looked expectantly up at Holmes.

"Delighted to join you, sir. And yes, Holmes, if you don't mind, pour me one as well."

Holmes paused and gave me one of those looks that passes between old friends when they take a good-natured poke at each other. Then he smiled and poured two fingers of Scotch into a glass.

"Mr. Bethune," Holmes said to me, "met me on the street only a minute ago. He brings news from Calcutta, which I expect both of us will find interesting. Mr. Bethune, sir, pray proceed."

"Four days ago, I received a brief telegram from Harish Sundaram, the young chap in our Calcutta office. He confirmed that substantial transfers of funds had been forwarded through the Bank of England to an account in the Bank of Calcutta. Those funds were then dispersed to ten local orphanages, all of whom are providing a modicum of care for destitute children."

He stopped and took a sip of his whiskey.

"He also stated that he had secured authority from the Administrative Office of the Raj to conduct a preliminary audit of the books of each of the orphanages and would be reporting back to me by the weekend."

He paused for another swallow.

"So far," said Holmes, "it appears that everything is on the up and up, does it not? Why then are you here this evening rather than waiting until the full audit report was received?"

"Because that report will not be sent. Mr. Sundaram is dead."

"Merciful heavens," I gasped. "What happened?"

"I am informed that on his way home from our office yesterday, he stopped to buy a few items in the New Market. Whilst there, he was set upon by a gang of thieves who stabbed and robbed him. The witnesses said that it happened very quickly and that he died almost immediately."

"The New Market?" said I. "When I was in India, it was said to be quite the stunning place. I never heard of its being dangerous."

"You are right, Doctor," said Bethune. "It isn't. Thousands of British men and women and the better-off Indians shop there every day. The merchants are very conscientious about keeping undesirables out. Their presence is bad for business."

"You are saying," said Holmes, "that he was deliberately followed and attacked, and, I assume, that you believe that his murder may have been connected to the task he had undertaken for us."

A feeling of horror swept over me. Mr. Bethune took another sip of his Scotch. Holmes sat impassively, waiting for him to answer.

"Yes, Mr. Holmes. It appears that we sent a man to his death."

"Come, come, now," I sputtered. "That cannot be certain. There could be a dozen other reasons why he was killed. Maybe he had a spat with his brother-in-law. Maybe there was a competition for the love of a young woman. Maybe there was a dispute over hereditary land somewhere in Bihar. Those Indian chaps are always doing each other in for any number of reasons."

Holmes gave me a bit of a look. "Those are all remotely possible. However, the probable cause, in most cases, is the most proximate. He was about to complete the task we gave him and send off his report. We may have failed to discern that we are dealing with ruthless men and not merely an exclusive band of Potemkin philanthropists."

For the next full minute, the three of us sat in silence. I felt my heart tighten in pain at the thought that a fine, young man was now dead as a direct result of his enthusiastic pursuit of the mission on which we had sent him. Holmes withdrew his cigarette case, lit one, took a long pull, and slowly exhaled.

"It is a terrible responsibility that weighs on anyone dedicated to the pursuit of justice. We can no more escape it than can Inspector Lestrade when he sends a constable to arrest a violent man, or when a general sends his young infantrymen into battle. Lives are lost, bodies are maimed, and families are ruined in the name of doing what is right. The greater failure is if we who bear that burden allow it to immobilize us. We have no choice, my friends. It is good to pause and reflect on the consequences of our actions—indeed of our failures. The much greater danger is our letting it stop our quest. We have to carry on."

He stubbed out his cigarette and looked at Mr. Bethune.

"Is there anything else to report, sir?"

"I admit that I am now puzzled concerning the use of the charity's funds."

"Explain, please."

"Have you been following the press concerning the election in America?"

"I confess," said Holmes, "that I have not. I equate the politics of America with the fantastical writings of Jules Verne. They are beyond my comprehension. What of them?"

"The wealthy bankers, the industrialists, the Boston Brahmins, the denizens of Wall Street—,"

"You are referring," said Holmes, interrupting Mr. Bethune, "to the Republican Party."

"Aye, those lads. They are all terrified of this William Jennings Bryan fellow. If he were to win the election for the Democrats and Populists, the Republican hold on the wealth and power of America could be shattered."

"Indeed, it would. And what has that to do with these fellows who may have been behind the murder of your man in Calcutta?"

"The Yankee potentates have unleashed every weapon in their arsenal. They are telling the populace that Bryan is Satan incarnate, a wanton brigand, a violater of Lady Liberty. Their tactics appear to be working, and there is now every indication that on the third of November, they will win, and McKinley will become the president."

"And the bimetallic movement will fail?" said Holmes.

"Yes. Their investing in silver will come to naught. They will lose a fortune, even if the funds are not their own. They read the press. They must know that. Yet they continue to invest in the silver-mining firms."

"That is curious," said Holmes. "No doubt, there is an explanation. Again. unfortunately, we have no idea what it is."

We chatted on for some time after that before Mr. Bethune departed, leaving me alone with Holmes.

"I would offer you another Scotch," he said to me, "but it is imperative that we have all our wits about us. Are you prepared to venture out?"

"Of course, I am, but would you mind telling me where to and what for?"

"To investigate that clubhouse in St. James Square. You remembered to bring your service revolver?"

"I did. And the rucksack."

"Excellent. I have a billy-club. Let us be off."

Chapter Fifteen

Trapped in the Basement

The midnight hour was approaching as Holmes and I found a cab to take us slowly through the fog and let us off on King Street. The streets were empty, and we walked up to St. James Square without seeing or being seen by anyone.

The street lamps illuminated no more than a radius of five yards, and the house that we planned to enter could not be made out until we were directly in front of it.

"On a night like tonight," he said, "I fancy I could pick the lock on the front door and never be disturbed. However, we must not throw caution to the winds. Come, Watson. We shall enter from the postern."

I held a match whilst Holmes used his hands and tools to open the door at the back of the house. Before the third match had burned down, he had released the lock, and we entered.

"Remove your shoes and put them in the rucksack," he whispered. "Silence is imperative. There are children here, and we must not disturb them."

Holding a lit candle in his hand, he found the half-staircase that led to the basement level. That floor consisted of a long, central hallway, with doors along each side. I had expected that it would feel dank and musty and that we might hear mice scurrying about. It was not like that. The floors were clean. The air was fresh.

One by one, Holmes opened the doors and peered in. The first half dozen were unlocked and used for various types of storage. Food in one, custodial supplies in another, empty steamer trunks in the next, and so on. I held the candle in each of these whilst Holmes conducted a silent, cursory search of the contents before concluding that there was nothing amiss.

The last two doors, just below the staircase beside the front door, were different. They were metal doors of the type a local bank might use to secure its vault.

"These doors are new," said Holmes. "The locks are from Chubb."

"Can you open them?"

"I expect so, but it may take me some time. May I count on you to hold the candles whilst I try?"

"I am your man."

"Excellent. Now, let me get to work."

I watched him in silence for twenty minutes. He jotted down one number, then the second, then the third. He looked up at me, smiling in triumph after recording the fourth and placed his hand on the vault handle. Then we both froze.

We heard the front door above us open, the quiet clattering of a carriage being unloaded, and voices.

"Into that storeroom," said Holmes. I blew out the candle, and we squeezed ourselves into a room that smelt of clean laundry and wool blankets. I pulled the door almost closed behind us, leaving only a small crack through which we could peer into the darkness. I crouched down, and Holmes, being taller, stood behind me as each of us pressed our face to the narrow, open slot.

I could hear snippets of different men talking quietly as they unloaded a carriage. "Easy now, it's heavy." "One of you on each corner." "Could you not have found a couple of peons for this?" "The fewer who know about what you do at night, the better."

This last comment was followed by a couple of muffled guffaws.

After several minutes of unloading at the door, they began bringing wooden cases down the basement stairs. The first case, a long, rectangular wooden box, arrived, and the four men carrying it stood still whilst a fifth man held a lantern with one hand and turned the vault dial with his other. The steel door swung open, and the fellows carrying the case wiggled and jogged their way through the door. We could not see what happened inside the room, but from the sound and muffled chatter, it was clear that they were hoisting the heavy case up and on to a pile of cases that were already there.

The five of them departed and climbed back up the stairs and prepared to bring another case down.

"Do you," whispered Holmes, "recognize the wooden case?"

"It's a rifle case. Last I saw one was during the war, but they are standard use in the armed forces."

"Precisely. I expect that smaller ammunition cases will follow."

He was right. It took them a full half-hour to bring four long boxes and half-a-dozen smaller ammunition cases into the vaults. Each longer case needed four chaps to carry, and the smaller cases took two. Judging by the grunts and the groans, it was hard work.

As they moved, they continued to exchange light-hearted whispers complaining about the weight along with some lewd comments of the type one might hear in a football clubhouse and a few absurdly snobbish remarks about physical labor not being an appropriate pastime for any Englishman and far better suited to those of darker skin color.

When the task had been completed, the five of them huddled together within earshot. The content was banal until one of them asked, "So, Doggie, what are we going to do about this Sherlock Holmes vermin?"

"Aye," said another. "He's a clever b—, he is."

"Your trap using those girls didn't get far. He saw it coming a mile off."

Several other comments were made that applied derogatory nomenclature to Sherlock Holmes and that I shall have to leave to the reader's imagination.

"We have Mr. Holmes all looked after," came the answer. "After Saturday night, you won't have to worry about him."

"What are you going to do?"

"He is going to have a Hallowe'en surprise. Tommy Todgers has rounded up a gang to pay him a visit, and if he can still walk and talk afterward, he'll have to be Lazarus come back from the dead."

"It's All Hallows Eve. Maybe his ghost will come back to haunt you, Doggie."

"You can't just knock on his door and attack him. He's too sharp to let that happen."

"No worries, my friend. A young damsel in distress—he cannot resist them—will knock on his door and beg his help for her son who was robbed of his soul cakes and is lying in the doorway across the street. Tommy and his boys will be waiting for him, and after that, he will have to be a ghost to ever do us harm again."

A round of chortles followed this last rejoinder, and the gang of them made their way upstairs. As best as I could tell, two of them departed the building, leaving three of them in the front entryway.

"There's a fortune in the basement," I heard one of them say. "Are you certain we do not need to hire a guard?"

"No. It would only draw attention. The vaults give us all the protection we need."

"Then we should at least check down here every so often, shouldn't we?"

"Not necessary. Go to bed. And be quiet. We don't want to wake up the urchins. I will see you in the morning."

We waited for another ten minutes, and then we inched our way back to the postern door and slipped out into the utter darkness of the London fog. In silence, we pulled our boots back on and walked north through the gloom until we found Piccadilly.

Chapter Sixteen

Return to the Empty House

Once inside a cab and working our way in the fog through Mayfair, I turned to Holmes.

"What sort of insurrection could they be planning? They cannot possibly be thinking of taking on the army or even the police. Surely, they cannot be that foolish. But they are collecting enough arms and ammunition to cause a serious disturbance."

"Do you believe that they are collecting arms and ammunition for their own use?"

"What else could they be doing? Or are they using funds raised for charity to ship arms to some rebel groups in India?"

"That is more probable but not at all certain."

"Then what is certain?"

"That I am to receive a beating on Saturday evening."

"Shall I have the honor of joining you?"

"If you could arrive by six, it would be useful. Dark clothes again. And your plimsolls."

"And my revolver?"

"If you don't mind."

The cab dropped us off at Baker Street. I finally went to my bed, leaving Holmes sitting and smoking in the parlor.

Late in the afternoon of 31 October, I sat down alone for an early supper, served graciously as always by the redoubtable Mrs. Hudson. I must have seemed ill at ease.

"Doctor," she said, placing a friendly hand on my shoulder. "You seem quite unsettled. Is there anything I can get you to help you relax?"

"No, but thank you, my dear lady. That is very understanding of you."

"What has Mr. Holmes put you up to this time?"

"Nothing either you or I would find surprising. He is going to receive a terrible beating at the hands of some dangerous miscreants, and he invited me to join him."

"Ah, so that is why he wanted me to help. Sounds quite smashing. Shall I fetch your cricket bat? It might be useful."

"Not necessary. I will have my service revolver with me."

"Oh, well, that is very reassuring."

By six o'clock, darkness had fallen, and Holmes returned to 221B Baker Street.

"How many are you expecting?" I asked him.

"Four or five ruffians. Thoroughly nasty fellows."

"There are only two of us."

"The Good Book tells us that the race is not to the swift, nor the battle to the strong."

"Perhaps not," said I, "but that is the way you place your bets. It has been a long time since I engaged in warfare, but I do remember that being outnumbered by two to one was not a good strategy. Two against five s not a wise plan of battle."

"To be more precise, it will be six or more against none. You and I will be on their side. Come, now, and get into disguise."

He retreated to the back hall of his rooms and returned, bearing a handful of theatrical items. Within twenty minutes, my eyebrows had added bushy volume and turned white, and I had a walrus mustache and eyeglasses. He had become unrecognizable with a shaggy mop of grey hair, sideburns, and an unkempt goatee.

"Put this on your head," he said, handing me a peaky blinders cap. "If you will carry this Penang lawyer, I shall take a single-stick. We have to appear as if we are ready to deliver a beating."

"Do we have names?" I asked. "I cannot imagine that you are going to introduce us as Holmes and Watson."

"Excellent reasoning, my friend. I shall be Ned Kelly, and you shall be John Wilkes Booth."

"But they are both dead."

"It is All Hallow's Eve. Their spirits have returned."

"Right. So, who are we going to beat?"

"Me … and you. Come."

At seven o'clock, we slipped out the back door of the house, through the yard, and into the alley that ran behind the houses on the west side of Baker Street. The miserable fog of earlier in the week had departed, and the night was clear and cool. As we neared the entrance to the Park, we heard and then saw several families with young children walking toward to open lawns where a bonfire had been lit and, judging by the hoots and laughter, games and bobbing for apples were already underway.

We crossed Baker Street and worked our way down the alley behind the houses on the east side until we reached a familiar wooden gate.

"I remember this place," I said to Holmes. It was indeed the same path by which he and I had entered the empty house that stood across the street from 221B Baker Street.

"This time," said Holmes, "Colonel Moran will not surprise us."

We passed through the vacant yard and into the same empty house as Holmes and I had hidden ourselves two years earlier. I started to tiptoe my way when Holmes stopped me.

"My dear Watson, we are the only ones in the house. There is no need for stealth. When our brothers-in-crime arrive, we shall want them to know that we are here."

"Oh, yes. I suppose that makes sense. When are you expecting them?"

"I had hoped they would be here already. I do not want to waste an entire evening waiting for them."

We ascended the stairs to the familiar vantage point, and we waited for half-an-hour.

"There they are now," said Holmes as we heard the back door open and the footsteps and voices of several men. Holmes walked over to the staircase.

"Hello, down there," he shouted. "Is that you, Tommy Todgers?"

All movement and chatter below us ceased. After a brief pause, an answer came.

Chapter Seventeen

We are Not Beaten

"Aye, it's me. Who the deuce are you?"

Holmes started to descend the stairs to the main floor and gestured to me to follow him.

"Hello there, chaps, ow am ya?" said Holmes affecting a Brummie accent. "Lord Dogsbody told me you'd be showing up and might need some 'elp. Name's Ned Kelly. This 'ere is me partner, John Booth."

"There's four of us already. Did he think we weren't tough enough?"

"Oh no. He knows you're right good and tough. He was worried you might not be smart enough."

"He what?"

"Well, you're taking on Mr. Sherlock Holmes, right?" said Holmes. "He's the cleverest bloke in London. Lord Doggie didn't want you to make a mess of it."

"Just who the blazes does he think he is? And who do you think you are pushing in on our work?"

"Don't be giving me a face as long as Livery Street, my good chap. We just get along, do what we was hired to do, and the money's good, and Bob's your uncle, right?"

The four of them exchanged some mumbles, and then Todgers replied.

"We don't like it, but if that's what's going on, then we'll go along."

"Ee-we-yar," said Holmes. "Where's your bab? We 'eard you was going to have one that would go and give a sob story to Sherlock Holmes to draw him over 'ere."

"She'll be along."

No sooner had he spoken than I heard another person enter from the back of the house and come toward us. In the soft glow from the street lamps that glimmered through the front window, I discerned a pale, attractive young woman who could not have been much beyond twenty years old.

"Nellie," said Todgers, "this here is Mr. Booth and Mr. Kelly. They've been sent to help us take care of our squire this evening."

She looked us up and down and did not give the impression of welcoming us.

"They're not cutting into our wages, are they?"

"No, His Lordship's American boy agreed to pay us each twenty pounds, and we'll hold him to that."

"Twenty?" said Holmes.

"Aye, twenty. What did he tell you?"

"He told us thirty."

"Bloody 'ell! There is no way you tell Johnny-come-lately he's getting ten bob more than we are."

He moved toward Holmes; his fist clenched in front of his chest.

"Ar, come now, there, sir," said Holmes. "We've no want to be unfair. Give us a note with your names and addresses, and as soon as we're paid, we'll bring three pounds to each of you. That'll make it all square. Our word on't."

He handed the fellow a notebook and a pencil, which were taken. But for a minute, Todgers stood still, and I imagined that I could hear the wheels turning inside his brain as he computed the arithmetic of what Holmes had promised. I sly smile crept across his face when he completed his mental task and realized that Holmes had agreed to give each of them six shillings more that he and I would receive.

"Right you are, then, Mr. Kelly. That's fair and decent. You can leave the money with the barkeep at *The Slug and Cabbage* in Spitalfields, and here's our names."

Holmes thanked him graciously, and Todgers turned to the young woman.

"Nelly, my pretty one. Time to go and do your role. Are you ready for it, dearie?"

"Aye. I have to go and ask for Mr. Holmes—,"

"No! You simpleton. You are not supposed to know that he lives there. You are only to ask if there is a gentleman living there who can help you."

"Oh, yes. I'll remember. And I say that my boy has been beaten and robbed of his soul cakes and that the boys who did it said they were coming back."

"Yes, Nellie. That's better. And try to look and sound hysterical. Can you do that."

"Aye, I can do that. What does *hysterical* mean?"

"Good Lord, woman. It means upset. Can you pretend to be upset?"

"Aye. I can be upset. But are you sure that Mr. Holmes is there?"

"Look across and into the window. See him?"

I looked across the street at the same time and stifled a gasp and a cry of amazement. The very same shadow of a man I had observed from this house two years ago was shown in hard, black outline upon the luminous screen of the window. I pulled Holmes back from the cluster of chaps standing by the door.

"Holmes," I whispered, "how did you plug the hole in the head?"

"Mrs. Hudson made up some bread dough. Fortunately, this time no one will shoot me. It would make a frightful mess."

The young woman departed the empty house, hurried across the street, and pounded loudly on the door. Then she appeared to be ringing the bell repeatedly. She kept it up for a full minute until the door opened, and the unmistakable shape of Mrs. Hudson appeared.

Nellie was gesticulating vigorously with her hands and arms, but Mrs. Hudson was not moving. I could not tell what she was saying to Nellie, but I assumed that she was pretending to be hard of hearing. Finally, she closed the door, leaving the distraught mother standing there.

The next thing we saw was the shadow of Holmes turning one way and then the other and then back again. He did not get up from his chair.

Mrs. Hudson reappeared, handed Nellie a note, and closed the door. Nellie took the note to the nearest street lamp and tried to read it before returning to the band of would-be miscreants in the empty house.

"Here you go, Todgers," she said on entering. "This is what he sent to me."

Todgers ordered one of his underlings to hold a match as he read it.

"Bloody 'ell. I can't believe it. That bleedin' toff says that he is 'frightfully busy examining a sixteenth-century score of American jazz and will along in due course.' Crikey! And they told us he would be all compassion and such for a young mother in distress. Now what do we do?"

"Perhaps," said Ned Kelly—also known as Sherlock Holmes, "we got to sit and wait. If he says he'll be along, then he'll be along, some time."

"Who does he think he is? We don't have all night to sit in this miserable place."

"Me train," said Holmes, "back to Birmingham don't leave till morning. Where's it you got to be?"

"I got to be home and in bed with the missus," said Todgers. His answer was echoed by two of the other men. "I've a good mind to tell

Lord Dogfleas that we'll deserve another one … no, make that two pounds each if we have to sit here in the cold for an hour."

An hour passed. Needless to say, Sherlock Holmes did not emerge from 221B Baker Street. His shadow, however, shifted once every quarter of an hour. After an hour and a half, Todgers uttered several oaths and called upon Nellie.

"Woman, get yourself back over there and weep and wail and do whatever it takes to get that arrogant snob to come and help you."

Nellie scampered across the street and again pounded on the door and rang the bell. Again, Mrs. Hudson appeared, but this time I could see that she had a small plate in her hand, which she thrust into Nellie's hands before closing the door in her face. Nellie stomped back across the street.

"That old dear gave me a plate of soul cakes and said to take them to my little boys. It will make them feel better."

"You mean *boy*," said Todgers.

"No. I may be poor, but I'm not deaf. She said *boys*. Like she knew what was going on. She even patted my hand and called me *dearie*."

"What the devil," cried Todgers. "We've been played. I've a mind to storm the door and give that bloke what he's got coming to him."

"Are you sure he's got no guns?" said Holmes-cum-Kelly. "I 'eard he was a bloody good shot wit a revolver and not afraid to use it."

Todgers paused. "Well, what are you gonna do then, Brummie?"

"My quarrel's not wit him. It's with the toff who sent me to stand here all night and be made a fool of. I'd say he's got to pay me forty pounds for the trouble. If'n I was you, I'd tell him the same thing."

"Bloody right, there, Brummie. That's what we'll do. First thing tomorrow morning, we'll pay a visit to St. Jimmy and demand our wage and something extra. You all in agreeance?"

We all exited to the pavement and stood briefly by the street lamp. Todgers and his gang walked south on Baker Street, but Nellie lingered behind. She gave a long look to Sherlock Holmes, and then a wisp of a smile appeared on her pretty face.

"Please thank the lady for the soul cakes. My mum and dad will enjoy them."

She stuffed the plate into her handbag and walked south. We waited until all of them were out of sight and crossed back to 221B. Holmes was positively giggling.

"Holmes," I admonished him. "Don't be so smug. Those blackguards are nasty fellows. They were prepared to send us to hospital."

"No doubt, my good doctor. And I fully expect that next time we shall not be threatened with a mere beating. But sufficient unto the day is the evil thereof. Come, a cup of tea before going to bed."

In the front room of 221B, Mr. Sherlock Holmes, cast in repaired plaster and returned from the dead, was sitting at the table. Mrs. Hudson had set out a pot of tea and a plate of soul cakes.

Chapter Eighteen

Supply and Demand

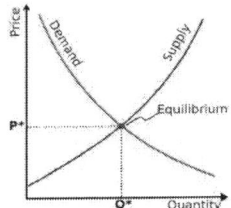

O n Tuesday, the third of November, the American populace went to the polls to elect their next president, and their congressmen, and their state senators, and their judges, and their water commissioners, and a dozen or more other civic officials. The results were wired across the Atlantic late the following day.

William McKinley and his Republicans defeated William Jennings Bryan and the combined forces of the Democratic and the Populist Parties.

The value of shares in silver mining enterprises plummeted.

"I suppose," I said whilst chatting with Holmes the following week, "that this puts paid to those St. James Square blokes trying to make a fortune off of silver. Their attempts to influence the election and elect a Democrat amounted to nothing."

"In comparison," said Holmes, "to the massive amounts of money spent by both opposing parties—those Americans who have and control wealth—they were utterly insignificant. I would have thought we had seen the end of their meddling, but I had a note from that Bethune chap. He asked if he could drop by for a chat. He should be along shortly."

Ten minutes later, the bell on Baker Street rang, and Mrs. Hudson dutifully led Mr. Marvin Bethune into the front room. He was accompanied by another much younger fellow whom I did not recognize but looked every bit as distinguished as the senior lawyer.

"Allow me, please," said Bethune, "to introduce Mr. Arthur Cecil Pigou. Please do not misjudge him because of his youth. He is a first-class economist and quite the expert on money, and the gold standard, and commodities and all those things."

Holmes shook the young man's hand and gestured to him to be seated.

"You have just returned from Switzerland, I see," said Holmes. "How was the climbing?"

He smiled back at Holmes.

"It was splendid, and I should have expected that Sherlock Holmes would say something like that, but I am at a loss to know how you did it. Please enlighten me, sir."

"Simplicity itself. I assure you it takes far less mental labor than understanding economics. But since you asked, I shall explain. Your face is tanned, but your ears and neck are not. The tan ends just before your hairline begins. That straight away rules out your having acquired the tan in a warm climate. One does not wrap one's head and neck with a hat and scarf in the tropics. Thus, you acquired your color from the wind and sun in a colder climate. The inevitable conclusion is that you were exposed to the elements whilst climbing. Your hands are highly calloused for an English gentleman. It is possible that you had been in Scotland climbing the Bens, but they do not require much technical climbing using the hands as well as legs and feet. Your lovely new cravat is made of Italian silk, and therefore it was safe to conclude that you recently returned from the Alps by way of Genoa. Now then, what is it that brought the two of you here today? Would you like a wee dram of Single Malt, Mr. Bethune, before responding."

"Aye, that would be grand."

I poured snifters of Scotch for all four of us, and, after a minute of serene sipping, Marvin Bethune replied.

"It is about the charity and the silver," he said.

"That much I would have assumed," said Holmes.

"The shares of the silver firms throughout the world have gone down in value."

"Of that I am also aware. The investments made in the name of the charity are now worth half as much as they were before the American election. The directors are guilty of poor judgment and stupidity. Those faults, however, are not crimes."

"Aye, 'tis true, if they were, we would have no parliament. But these chaps were not as foolish as we had at first believed."

"Explain, please, sir."

"They did not buy shares in silver mining and processing firms with that money."

"Then what did they buy?"

"They bought silver," said Bethune.

"They bought the metal itself?" asked Holmes. "No one does that, do they?"

Bethune nodded to the young economist, and he answered.

"No, sir. What they buy are contracts for future delivery of the silver, not the metal itself. Those contracts may be sold and re-sold several times before they divided up into smaller and smaller units and eventually sold to silversmiths throughout the world. They, in turn, turn the silver into plate and jewelry and objects of ornamentation."

"Wherein is the problem?" said Holmes.

"The flow of silver contracts throughout the metal exchanges of the world has vanished. Not a contract has been sold, and no silver delivered to any smith for the past two months. All delivery of silver bars and finished plate to the London Silver Vaults in Chancery Lane have ceased. The movement of silver throughout the world has dried up. No one knows where it has gone. These fellows from St. James Square have acquired it and have hidden it somewhere."

Holmes leaned back in his chair as a smug smile crept across his face.

"I believe you will find it all in the basement of their clubhouse," said Holmes. "Watson and I watched them carry it in a few nights ago."

Messrs. Bethune and Pigou were surprised, and I was dumbfounded.

"But those," I protested, "were military rifle and ammunition cases."

"My dear Watson," said Holmes, "that was my first impression as well. But you served in Her Majesty's army. How many men does it take to carry a full case of rifles?"

"Usually, two."

"And an ammunition case?"

"One ... Ah ha! They needed four of them to carry the big case, and two for the small ones and they were huffing and sweating whilst doing so. Far too heavy to be rifles. Were those cases full of silver bullion?"

"Precisely, Watson. Now, gentlemen, we can see what these fellows are doing. It is very odd behavior and possibly a violation of their fiduciary duty to the trust, but wherein is the crime? And why would both a young woman from London and an auditor in Calcutta be murdered, as we assume they were?"

"That, Mr. Holmes," said Bethune, "is why we are here. We don't know."

"If I may, gentlemen," said the younger man. "It appears that these men may be much cleverer than you at first believed. In the event of the defeat of the Democrats in America—a result they very likely expected—that they had a much more ambitious plan in store."

"And what do you deduce that to be?"

"Well, sir, silver is a commodity, and like all goods and services, its price is affected by the law of supply and demand. I refer you to the work of Professor Alfred Marshall of Cambridge, under whom I am privileged to study. In his recent *Principles of Economics,* he explained how the value of almost any good or service will increase when the demand for it increases, and the supply remains constant or decreases. If the supply of silver to the world is cut off, but the demand remains the same, these men will have cornered the market, and the cost of silver will be driven up two, five, or even ten-fold."

"In which situation," said Holmes, "the value of the silver in the basement of the house on St. James Square will increase greatly in value. This would suggest that these men have been astute and even brilliant in their management of the funds entrusted to them."

"But only," I said, "if all that value is used to help the children in Calcutta and does not end up in their pockets."

"True," said Holmes, "but at present, we have no evidence of such fraud, and thus no motive for what we suspect were the murders of Miss Westbury and Mr. Sundaram. All we have is conjecture based on our instincts, and, likely correct though they may be, it remains a capital mistake to act before acquiring sufficient data."

"Is there nothing," I said, "that can be done?"

"There may be," said Mr. Bethune. "Both the Bank of England and the professors of Cambridge University have some influence on Her Majesty's Cabinet and at Number Eleven."

"Then what," I asked, "are you going to do?"

"England's politicians, since the time of the Corn Laws until the present, have shown a remarkable capacity to enact laws and regulations that strangle unwanted innovation in industry and commerce. I expect we can count on the current lot to do likewise."

"All well and good," said Holmes, "but it does nothing to address the likely murder of two innocent young lives."

"That," said Mr. Bethune, "is your territory, Mr. Homes, not ours. All I can suggest is that you damn the data and move full speed ahead on your instincts."

Chapter Nineteen

Violet is Patient but Not for Long

A golden October had declined into somber November. Leaves had fallen. Mild sunny days were gone, and frost had appeared several times on the pavement. Once a fortnight, Holmes paid a visit to the Westbury home in Chelsea and gave the family a candid report on the results of his investigation. I went with him and immediately noticed that the striking portrait of Miss Isabella Westbury had been removed from the entrance to the family home in Chelsea, along with the bouquets of flowers sent in condolence. Our meetings were somber affairs.

The three Westbury family members agreed to keep everything Holmes told them in strictest confidence, and he let them know about the shipments of silver stored in the basement of the house, and the failed attempt at giving him a beating. The mother and grandfather found the account amusing. Violet did not.

As we were leaving the house after the second meeting, Mr. Paterson pulled on his overcoat and came out onto the street with us.

"Mr. Holmes," he said, "I can see that you are being very diligent. Violet's mother and I are no longer young, and so we understand that these things take time, and when justice is rushed it is in danger of failing. But Violet is young. She is impatient. She has made up her mind that these men murdered Isabella, and she is consumed with seeing them arrested and tried. Please do not be offended by her impatience."

"I cannot be impatient with her," said Holmes, "because I have the very same feelings. It is terribly frustrating, but these men are not fools. They are biding their time and have given me no cause yet to have the police lay charges against them. But they will not wait forever. And when they act, we shall pounce."

"This, I understand," said the elderly gentleman. "my only prayer is that they will hang before I am required to move into the next life."

I was not at all sure that the Almighty was responsive to such prayers, but I knew that if Holmes had been in the habit of offering prayers, he would have troubled Heaven with the same request.

The directors of the charity were not in a hurry. Encouraged by the success of the concert at the Royal Albert Hall, the Society for the Care of Street Orphans had organized a tour of the Chorale of Angels and were conducting similar concerts in Birmingham, Manchester, Liverpool, and Glasgow all before Christmas. The reviews in the press were glowing. In addition to attending the concert and pledging a monthly donation to the Society, patrons could also purchase commemorative plates, wall plaques, medallions, tea towels, and picture books, all filled with the likeness of Miss Isabella Westbury and tributes to and anecdotes of her young life. She had been credited with composing several sentimental prayers for children, all of which were a slim notch above *Now I Lay Me Down to Sleep,* and these were made available in numerous formats and sizes from a thimble to a wall hanging.

I might have asked Sherlock Holmes his opinion of this enterprise, but I saw very little of him. I had no doubt he was hard at work on this case, but it was not until the end of the month that I heard from him again. A note sat on the breakfast table telling me that the family of Isabella Westbury had requested a further meeting, and he asked that I join him.

A maid ushered Holmes and me into the parlor, where we were greeted by the grandfather, Mr. Paterson, the mother, and Miss Violet Westbury. After the required few minutes of asking after their well-being and their expected response that they were bearing up during these trying times, they came to the point of their invitation.

"We have finally completed a sad but necessary task." said Mr. Paterson, "We have sorted and cleared out Isabella's clothes and belongings. Doing so has been very painful for us, but it had to be done, and the items given to charity will, we pray, assist a poor family. It is what we know Isabella would have wanted us to do."

"I am certain," I said, "that the recipients will be thrilled to receive the gifts. Your granddaughter was a very fashionable young woman."

"And I am certain," said Holmes, who had already been glancing at his watch, "that you did not call us to meet with you so that you could give us one of her dresses or even her books. I do not wish to be tactless, but time is of the essence in this case, and I assure you I am working diligently to determine the possibility of criminal actions and bring villains, if they exist, to justice. Kindly explain your purpose in asking us to meet with you again."

The old man smiled at Holmes. I assumed that he had not gone from being a butcher's apprentice to a wealthy man of business by letting the grass grow under his feet.

"Of course, sir," he said. "We asked you to meet with us because of something we found in Isabella's possessions. She kept accurate, up-to-date files of her notes and correspondence. Several of the files related to the work of the Calcutta charity. Most were copies of minutes, flyers, publicity brochures, and such, but there was one that struck us as interesting, and that we wished you to see."

He handed a file over to Holmes. It appeared to contain copies of correspondence and of telegrams sent and received. He read one page after another, handing them over to me as soon as he had finished. Mrs. Westbury, the mother, organized a round of tea, and we sipped and read for the next fifteen minutes.

The letters and telegrams had all been marked "personal and confidential" and had been sent by Isabella Westbury to ten of the affiliated homes and shelters for children in Calcutta. All of the homes were asked to confirm the receipt of the funds forwarded through the Bank of Calcutta and give a detailed account of how those funds were used. Every one of the homes replied in a timely manner, and indeed confirmed they had received the designated funds. They further stated that the money had been used to purchase food, school uniforms, medicines, play clothes, and sanitary supplies. Their doing so was in keeping with the report Mr. Bethune had received through Harish Sundaram before his unfortunate end.

There was one problem.

Included in the itemized list of disbursement of each home was an entry amounting to three percent of the funds received that was paid by wire to an account in a Swiss Bank, *Debit Suisse* in Zurich. It was noted as an "international transfer fee."

"Please tell me, Mr. Holmes," said the grandfather, "does that entry raise suspicion? I am now an old man, and I do not claim any expert knowledge of how money is sent around the world today, but I always thought that the fee was taken off at the start by the bank that sent the funds. Is that not how it works today?"

"It is," said Holmes.

"And I also learned many years ago that if money was sent through a Swiss bank, it was because someone had something to hide. Is that still true today?"

"Not always, but quite often. Yes."

"Violet noticed it when we she looked at the file, and she showed it to me. It may be entirely legitimate, but it had that faint odor of not-quite-right to it. Would you agree, Mr. Holmes?"

"I would, and I shall investigate it. As you say, it may be entirely proper, and, then again, it may not."

"Thank you, sir. I hope we have not taken up too much of your time."

"Not at all."

We stood and prepared to depart when Miss Violet Westbury stopped us.

"Mr. Holmes. I am frankly not interested in knowing whether or not these men are taking a few pounds away from the children and putting it in their pockets. What I want to know is if they killed my sister, and if they did, are they going to hang for it?"

"Now, Violet," began her grandfather. "The police—,"

"No, grandpa. I will not be content to leave it to the police. I have not shut an eye since the tragedy, thinking, thinking, thinking, night and day, what the true meaning of it can be. I hired Sherlock Holmes to find out what happened to Isabella. And I will not be content until I am assured by him that justice has been done."

"Miss Westbury, I did not rest until I discovered what happened to your fiancé, and I assure you, I will not rest until I learn the truth of what happened to your sister. On that, you have my promise."

Once we had departed the house, I queried Holmes.

"That three percent item, can it truly be material? Goodness knows what fees have to be paid in India. When I was there, the Raj was an expert at finding ways to shake the pennies and shillings out of everyone. Three percent is nothing."

"No, Watson. Three percent is a test."

"A what?"

"Any time a firm or an individual opens a new conduit for the transfer of funds across international borders, it is a prudent and indeed necessary first step to send a small amount the first time to prove that the chosen banks and agents are reliable. I fully suspect that future transfers will require increasing levels of fees to be paid back. Unfortunately, I have no choice but to wait and see."

Sherlock Holmes did not like to wait. Patience was one of the many human virtues he lacked. Fortunately, he did not have to wait long. The next event, however, did not come as an arrest, or a great discovery of evidence. It came in the form of a small notice tucked into the back pages of the *Financial Times*.

Chapter Twenty

Don't Bring a Knife to a Gun Fight

The Financial Times

TUESDAY, 1 DECEMBER   EVENING EDITION

Notice from Chancellor of the Exchequer

A minor amendment to the Coinage Act of 1870 has been proposed. In response to the Royal Guild of Silversmiths' submission demonstrating exceptional irregularities in the world supply of silver, Her Majesty's Government is contemplating an amendment to the above Act that would give the Royal Mint the power to compel suppliers of silver bullion to sell their entire stock to the Mint at current market prices. The Mint will then allocate regular quarterly transfers to registered silversmiths. Interested parties wishing to comment on this amendment are invited to submit written suggestions to the Office of the Chancellor before five o'clock p.m., 10 December 1896. No submissions will be accepted after that time.

As I am not in the habit of spending much time reading about finance and commerce, I read the notice quickly and moved on. Then I stopped and read it again.

"Good heavens," I said to Holmes as we sat by the hearth. "Was this the doing of that Bethune fellow? He's retired now, isn't he?"

"He is," said Holmes, "which means he has many years of favors owed. Not to mention the brilliance of that young chap, Pigou."

"Him? But he is still a student," I said.

"One," said Holmes, "who needs to be watched. Mark my words, Watson, he is on his way to the top."

I shrugged and moved on to the sporting news. Having exhausted those pages, I set about cleaning my service revolver and prepared to pack it away, hoping that I would have little use of it now that Advent was upon us. Holmes lit his pipe and returned to some journal of criminology that had arrived in the day's post. I was about to get up and pour us both a brandy when we heard cries coming from somewhere south of us on Baker Street.

"MR. HOLMES! DOCTOR WATSON! OPEN YOUR DOOR. OPEN YOUR DOOR!"

The cries were repeated and came closer. Someone was running quickly toward 221B and was desperate. I bounded up and fumbling with my revolver, managed to load two cartridges into it, and rushed toward the stairs. Holmes was already ahead of me and, with his long, agile legs, descended the stairs two or three at a time. Whoever it was that was crying for our help had already pounded on our door. Holmes threw it open, and a man bounded past us and leapt up the stairs.

"Close the door!" he shouted. "They have knives!"

A knife is a poor thing up against a gun, and so I stepped out onto the pavement just as four men came rushing toward me. I lifted the gun and fired it into the air above them.

They stopped.

Sherlock Holmes stepped out in front of me and stood in front of the men.

"Do what you were told. Be gone now."

"We just need to have a wee chat with the fellow who ran inside."

"No Tommy Todgers, Freddie Deeming, Ikey Solomon and Christopher Theakstone, you do not need to speak to him. Now, run along before I call a constable and turn you over for committing criminal assault and battery."

"We never laid a finger on him and … hey, how did you know our names?"

"My name is Sherlock Holmes, and it is my business to know things. Now, be gone, and if you should ever return, Dr. Watson will not shoot over your heads."

They gave each other puzzled looks and turned and shuffled back south on Baker Street, muttering to each other.

"How did he—,"

"Aye, how the 'ell did he know who—,"

"That Brummie! The one what called himself John Booth. He must have told him. I knew you couldn't trust those Brummies. They're all double-crossers, not an honest thief among the lot of them."

"But he give us our three pounds each."

"Don't make no difference. Like as not, he then went right to Sherlock Holmes and sold us out for another tenner."

"Aye, that must have been what happened. Bloody Brummies."

I climbed back up the steps with a grin on my face and was about to say something jovial when I walked into the front room and looked on the pale, disheveled Mr. Arthur Pigou sitting on the sofa. His lip was swollen, and a black eye was forming. I went straight away to the mantle and poured a generous snifter of brandy and thrust it into his trembling hands.

Holmes spoke to him. "Your very first run-in with the criminal class of London, eh, Mr. Pigou?"

The young man took a large swallow and several deep breaths. "It was. I was not expecting it."

"What happened?"

"I was taking a stroll in Regent's Park and was not far from the entrance from Baker Street when suddenly those four men set upon me. I was manhandled and punched, and then they held a knife to my face and made some very vile threats."

He took another gulp of brandy.

"I'm sorry," he said. "I must be in shock. I was very frightened."

"But you broke free," said Holmes. "Well done."

"Yes, I suppose I had the presence of mind to know that I had to get away from them, so I twisted out of their grip and ran for my life. Your house was the closest one I knew, and so I started shouting for you. Thank God, you were here and came to my rescue."

"And did the threats they made against you have anything to do with your recent activities connected to the regulation of silver bullion."

"Well, yes. But how did you know that?"

I was quite sure that Holmes was about to say *My name is Sherlock Holmes and* ... so I took it upon myself to answer.

"I read the notice in *The Financial Times*. It had your fingers all over it, young man. Quite impressive."

"Oh, well, thank you, Doctor. It wasn't really much my doing. Mr. Bethune and Professor Marshall arranged a meeting with Sir Michael Beach at Number Eleven, and they told me to come along in case they needed me to quote some facts and figures."

"How did you get Beach to go along?" said Holmes. "He's a Conservative and hates having the government interfere with the free conduct of commerce."

"That is true, sir. But there are several large silversmith factories in Bristol. That is his riding, and Mr. Bethune contacted them, and they sent Sir Michael a letter reminding him of the votes of all the employees and shareholders, and then he was quite amenable to our suggestions."

"Brilliant," said Holmes. "And you have learned the first lesson of political life."

"What is that?"

"No matter what you do, you will make enemies."

"Oh my, I'll say. These thugs were nasty. But they cannot be the men from that St. James Club."

"Merely hirelings. Our toffs would not risk scratching their own knuckles. They prefer to buy such services. What they will do, however, is use their connections to attempt to make sure that the changes to the Coinage Act do not pass."

"But how?"

"They all went to Harrow."

"Oh, yes, right. But at least they went to Oxford after that and not Cambridge."

"If you believe that makes a difference, I fear you may be in for a second lesson in the near future," said Holmes.

Arthur Pigou sighed and slowly and painfully stood up.

"Again, gentlemen," he said. "Thank you. As I plan to pursue a career in political economy, do you have any more advice?"

"Get a gun," said Holmes.

Chapter Twenty-One

Interrogating the Little Ones

The days passed as Christmas approached. The Isabella Westbury Concerts continued to attract wildly enthusiastic audiences as the Chorale of Angels filled halls in the major cities of Britain. With the coming of Christmas, the program was altered, and some of the hymns and patriotic songs were replaced with songs of the season and Christmas carols. A live donkey had been acquired, and Mary and Joseph, Baby Jesus, shepherds with tea towels strapped around their heads, and wise men in Sikh turbans replaced the composite Union Jack. One of the smallest boys bade the audiences a farewell by squeaking a heartfelt, "God bless us, everyone." The great English proletariat loved it.

Indeed, the entire country had entered into the spirit of yuletide. Smiles were everywhere.

Sherlock Holmes was miserable. Both his investigation of the two deaths and of the questionable transfer of funds had been frozen in place.

On Friday, the eighteenth of December, one week before Christmas, the two of us were in the front room of 221B. I was reading and enjoying a cup of tea. Holmes was pacing … and pacing … and pacing.

"My dear Holmes," I finally said. "There is no point being agitated. Nothing is going to happen until after the New Year. You may as well throw the burden off your shoulders until then. Why don't you read something, play something on your violin, or write a monograph on the scientific identification of body hair."

"Why don't I, Watson? Is that what you are asking me? I will tell you why. I will not relax because two young lives have been snuffed out, and my actions contributed to one of them. Because the killers are still at large. Because a massive fraud is in the works. And I have not a scrap of evidence that will stand up in court and can do nothing to stop more vile events from unfolding. That is why."

"Holmes, it's almost Christmas. Even criminals take time off. Unless you can somehow force their hand, they will do nothing until Epiphany has come and gone."

I harrumphed and settled back into my chair and dropped my gaze into my book. Holmes just stood still as a statue and glared at me.

"Watson, my dear chap, have I ever told you that there are some rare occasions when you are utterly brilliant?"

I looked up. He was smiling warmly, and there had not been a scintilla of sarcasm in his voice.

"Was that a compliment, Holmes?"

"It was, yes, it was. I shall have to force their hand. I shall have to do something that will cause them to act. And I shall have to do it immediately. Yes, that is just the thing. Thank you, Watson. Sometimes you are truly useful beyond being a scribe."

He started pacing again but now was moving almost at the speed of a forced march.

He stopped.

"AH HA!"

"What now, Holmes?"

He marched over to the bay window and looked out.

"The winter solstice is almost upon us. It will be completely dark within the next hour. Come, Watson. Pull on some black clothing. The game is afoot."

"And bring my service revolver?"

"Good heavens, no. They're only children."

An hour later found us on King Street and walking toward St. James Square. We slipped silently into the alley along the side of the unnamed club building until we were entirely hidden in the dark. Holmes laid his hand on my forearm and bade me stop. We waited until our eyes became accustomed to the lack of light. In the tiny glimmer that filtered in from the street, I could now make out the shape of a body standing a few yards in front of us. Holmes tugged on my arm, and we inched forward until we were immediately behind the sentry.

"Halloa Bulldog!" said Holmes somewhat more loudly than was necessary.

"WWHHAAA!!" the young man shrieked, and he jumped a foot in the air. It is a good thing that the hearts of young men do not succumb to sudden shocks, or Bulldog would have expired on the spot.

"At ease, Bulldog," said Holmes. "We come in peace."

"Oh, Mr. Holmes, oh. You gave me a fright. Where did you come from?"

"From Baker Street. What has happened here so far this evening?"

"Uh … umm … nothing yet, sir. The rest of us, your Irregulars, are stationed on the other side of the building. The boys and girls from the Chorale will be slipping through the window come seven o'clock."

"Why? Are there plans for the night?"

"Well, sir, we promised we'd take them to see the Christmas Market over in Leicester Square. They're right excited about it, sir."

"Who is going with you? All of the senior boys and girls?"

"Rights, them's coming, but so are the little ones."

"You are taking the children across London at night?"

"It's no more than we do all the time with the youngest of your Irregulars, sir. They're awful looking forward to it. Jumping up and down, they were when we told them. It's their first night out with us. You might say it's our Christmas present to them. Mind you, sir, most of them are Hindus and don't know aught about Baby Jesus and such, but the lights and the treats and the magic shows will be quite the treat for them, sir."

"Splendid," said Holmes. "I need to meet with the entire group of them before you leave."

"All at once, sir?"

"Yes."

"Oh, we can't do that, Mr. Holmes."

"And, pray tell, why not?"

"That would be a crowd of over twenty. You never move in such a crowd through the West End of London. Every copper on the street would stop you and give you you-know-what. We always move just in small groups so as not to arouse attention."

Holmes paused. "How very clever. Very well then, bring them out a few at a time and take them into St. James Square. Wait under the trees behind the statue of King William until they are all assembled. I will meet with them there. Can you do that, Master Bulldog?"

"Oh, right, sir, I suppose we can. But please don't be keeping the little ones too long. They're chomping at the bit to go to the Christmas Market."

Half-an-hour later, Holmes and I were standing in front of the sixteen members of the Chorale of Angels and a half-dozen strapping members of the Baker Street Irregulars. A light snow had begun to fall, and the temperature had fallen to below freezing.

Master Bulldog whispered to Holmes. "Please don't keep them too long, sir. The little ones need to get moving before they start to shiver. They're not at all fond of our English weather. They thought maybe you were going to come with us like as you did on the criminal walk, and they were quite sad when I said you only wanted to talk to them."

Holmes turned to the boys and girls. "Kindly listen up, children. I shall not keep you for long. I need all of you to think back all the way to October and try to remember what took place in the time just after you came to England. Each week four of you paid a visit to Lord Dalgingham's lovely big home. Do you all remember that?"

There was a round of affirmative murmurs and nods.

"Splendid. Now then, I need to know which boys and girls were there when Miss Isabella met her tragic death. I know it was very shocking for all of you, but I have to know which ones among you were staying at the house that week."

There was another round of murmurs and chatter, and one of the older boys stepped forward.

"I can tell you that, Mr. Holmes. My name is Rajiv, and I made very very sure to gather all the data I can whenever anything untoward takes place. I made careful notes of everything I heard that week."

"Excellent, Rajiv. You will make a superb detective someday."

"Oh, thank you, sir. Thank you. And yes, I can tell you straight away that during that very very sad week the members of our chorale who were staying at the house were four of our younger ones. The girls were Prisha and Ishana, and the boys were Parv and Zuber. Come now! The four of you. Come and stand in front of Mr. Holmes. Hurry, hurry. Spit, spot."

Four children emerged from the group, all of whom could not have been more than nine or ten years old.

"Excellent," said Holmes. "The rest of you may leave now, one small group at a time, and join up again at the Christmas Market. These ones will be along later."

The four children were looking daggers at Sherlock Holmes. They were clearly not at all happy about being kept behind. Holmes read the look and their faces.

"Now, now. I know it was not fair," he said, "to keep you behind. But because you have been, you will be given a special reward. Dr. Watson will give each of you a shilling to spend at the market. That seemed to satisfy three of them, but the fourth, the boy who identified as Parv, spoke up.

"Mr. Holmes, sir, it is not just that we are being kept late, it is also that it is cold here in the trees. Would you mind making our reward two shillings instead?"

Holmes looked at the lad and smiled.

"Tell me, Parv, is your father a merchant?"

"Yes, sir. He trades with Englishmen all day long, every day."

"You have a bright future ahead of you, Parv. So, yes, Dr. Watson will give you each two shillings, but only if you answer all my questions as completely as you can. Are we agreed on that?"

They all nodded, although one of the girls cast a glance at the last group of her friends who were now leaving the square.

"Brilliant. Now then, each of you think back to the day you were at Lord Peter's house, and you learned that Miss Isabella had died. Can you all remember that day?"

Nods.

"Think back to your lunchtime. What did you do after lunch?"

"Straight away after lunch?" asked Prisha.

"Yes."

"We all had to go to our bedrooms and have a nap. And we all did that."

"Excellent. Now then, after your nap, what did you do?"

Prisha turned to Ishana and whispered. "Did we go down to the library to practice our song?"

Ishana nodded.

"We went to the library to practice our song. We sang *I've Been Working on the Railroad*."

"And why did you do that?" asked Holmes.

"Because we had to perform it for the men from the Society."

"And for Miss Isabella," said Parv.

"Yes, yes," said Ishana. "And for Miss Isabella."

"And did you? Did you perform it for them?" asked Holmes.

Nods.

"When did you do that?"

"Just before supper," said Zuber, who up to this time had said nothing. "it was five o'clock when we went up to the roof terrace to sing for them."

"To the roof?" said Holmes.

"Yes, sir. They were all together up there. They were drinking some wine and eating some treats before dinner. We had some as well.

They were very tasty, I remember. But only the treats. We did not have any of the wine."

"Do you remember who was there with you on the roof terrace?"

"Oh, yes, sir. There was Uncle Timothy, and Uncle Peter, and Uncle Decimus, and Uncle Montague, and Uncle Oliver."

"And Miss Isabella," said Prisha.

"Yes, yes. And Miss Isabella."

"Were there any maids or servants?" asked Holmes.

The children looked at each other and then started shaking their heads.

"No, sir," said Zuber. "I do not remember seeing any of the servants there."

"Nor do I," added Parv.

"Very well, then. What happened after you had enjoyed your treats?"

"We sang our song," said Prisha, "and then we departed and went back down the stairs."

"Did one of the men or Miss Isabella go with you?"

"One of the uncles came with us. I believe it was Uncle Decimus," said Parv.

"No," said Prisha, "it was Uncle Oliver."

"On yes, yes. It was he. He took us to the kitchen where the cook had a special dessert for us. Yes, yes, that is what we did."

"And you waited there until suppertime? Is that right?"

"Yes, sir," said Prisha. "But I remember that we waited a long time and that it was quite late before the maid, Miss Smoot, came and helped the cook serve our supper but we ate supper in the kitchen with the servants, and Miss Smoot waited until we had finished our supper, and that was when she told us about Miss Isabella, and then we went back up to our rooms and the next day we were taken back to London."

For an entire minute, Holmes said nothing, and I could see that the children were becoming very restless and impatient. I gave him a nudge and leaned toward his ear.

"Is that all, Holmes?"

"Oh, yes. No, no. One more question, children. When you were on the roof, did all of the adults seem to be happy?"

"Yes," said Parv. "They were all very happy. They had been drinking wine, and that made them happy."

"No, Parv," said Ishana. "They were not all happy. Miss Isabella was very vexed. She did not even clap or smile when we finished our song. All of the girls were very fond of her, and I watched her whilst we were singing. She had a frown of her face, and when all the men applauded at the end of the song, she only patted her hands together twice. I was upset because I thought she was not pleased with our song."

"Yes, yes," added Prisha. "I remember that. She always smiled at us, and that afternoon she did not smile."

Holmes paused again and then thanked them. "That was very helpful. Thank you. Dr. Watson will give you each two shillings, and you can be on your way to the Christmas Market."

"Mr. Holmes, sir," said Parv.

"Yes, Parv."

"This took much much longer than we thought it would. Do you not think we should receive three shillings?"

The four of them, accompanied by one of the irregulars, trotted off in the direction of Leicester Square. Their pockets were jingling, and mine were empty.

"I dare say, Holmes, you owe me a pound on that one."

"It was worth every farthing. Now comes our next move."

"And what would that be?"

"The St. James boys asked me to conduct a thorough investigation. I did, and I shall make my report to them. I think Sunday would be a good time. Fancy an interesting afternoon in the Strangers' Room?"

Chapter Twenty-Two

Reporting to the Directors

Sherlock Holmes was up and gone before I appeared in 221B on Sunday morning. A note left for me requested my presence at the Diogenes Club for a meeting at two o'clock in the afternoon.

I arrived at one-thirty. The porter showed me into the Strangers' Room and offered me a selection of Ports, whiskeys, and cigars. I elected to take soda water.

A meeting table had been set up with chairs posted around it. A large armchair with a side table sat in the corner. At five minutes to two, Mycroft Holmes entered and grunted in my direction. He dropped his massive frame into the armchair which, I hoped, had been sufficiently reinforced to handle a sudden impact of twenty stone. A member of the club staff appeared almost immediately and placed a glass of Port on the side table and a nearly full bottle of the same beside it.

"Watson," said Mycroft, "wake me up when the rest of this puppet show arrives." He sloped into the chair and closed his eyes.

At a quarter past two, I heard Holmes's voice in the hallway.

"This way, please, gentlemen. We are meeting in this room. Kindly take a seat at the table. The staff will be along with whatever refreshments you might desire, and the spirits and snacks are excellent.

Ah, good afternoon, Dr. Watson. You do remember meeting Lord Dalgingham and Mr. Olleitch. Joining them are the directors of the society, Mr. Decimus Fernsby, Baron Montague Fitz Leigh, and Mr. Oliver Glasshover. And gentlemen, my friend and colleague, Dr. Watson."

They gave me a quick look but fixed their gaze on the massive hulk reposed in the corner.

"Ah, yes," said Holmes. "And that is my esteemed older brother, Sir Mycroft Holmes, who does a bit of this and that over in Whitehall and has been invaluable to me in preparing my report to you. Please, make yourselves at ease. Enjoy the refreshments before we get down to business."

Mycroft opened one eye and closed it again.

"Mr. Holmes," began Lord Peter Dalgingham, "We are here in answer to your insistence that we attend. We admire your energy and industry, but, frankly, I see no reason for the rush. This could have been postponed until after the New Year. We really—,"

"Tit, tut, now, Lord Peter. You commissioned me to carry out an investigation and report to you. It is my manner to deliver a report with alacrity immediately my work is completed. Unlike gentlemen in your situation, I do not enjoy independent wealth, and I still have to sing for my supper. I have other cases in the offing, and each day I do not work on them is a day in which I am not paid. I appreciate your understanding and indulgence."

He stopped and looked up at the door of the room.

"Ah, our final attendee has arrived. Good afternoon, Inspector Lestrade of Scotland Yard."

Lestrade entered and dropped into one of the chairs at the table. Two constables in uniform followed him and stood on either side of the door. The look on the faces of the directors of the Society was priceless.

"My dear Inspector," said Holmes, "would you care to introduce yourself?"

"You just did, Holmes. Get on with it."

"Mr. Holmes!" sputtered Lord Peter. "what is Scotland Yard doing here? We hired *you* to investigate the incident, not Scotland Yard."

"Oh, come, come, my dear chap. If I am hired to look after a case, I have no choice but to deliver the finest possible product to my client. It would be one thing for you to have a report fully exonerating your good selves and the Society that was signed by yours truly. But I am merely a consulting detective. Think of how much more weight the report will carry if it bears the *imprimatur* of Scotland Yard. I would not think of providing valued clients with anything less than the best possible return for their investment, and Scotland Yard's stamp on every page adds enormous value to what is about to be delivered. Is that not right, Inspector Lestrade?"

Lestrade looked at Holmes sideways. "Right, Holmes."

"But surely," said Timothy Olleitch, "he did not have to bring uniformed police officers along. What do you think is going to happen?"

Lestrade answered that question himself. "These two officers are in training to become inspectors. So, for this entire month, they have to follow me like a shadow everywhere I go. Their names are Linseed and Mallowford."

As he named them, he pointed with his thumb first over his left shoulder and then his right. And then added, "You can just ignore them."

The one identified as officer Mallowford already had a notebook and pencil in his hand and was busy scribbling notes.

"Excellent," said Holmes, "now let us get on with it. Allow me to begin by assuring my clients that I conducted a complete and thorough investigation of any and all matters that could possibly pertain to the tragic death of Miss Isabella. Oh, but before I start on that, forgive me as I would be remiss if I did not extend to all of you my condolences on your loss of a dear colleague and friend. And my personal sympathies to you, Lord Dalgingham."

Lord Peter looked confused. "What for?"

"Well, sir, because she was your sister, was she not?"

His Lordship eyes widened, but he recovered instantly. "My step-sister, yes. We were not raised together and were not close in any familial way."

Decimus Fernsby and Oliver Glasshover were giving Lord Dalgingham a strange look. Apparently, this was news to them.

Dalgingham forced a smile back at Holmes.

Lestrade was giving His Lordship a hard look. The Inspector had been around long enough to know that whenever there was a significant inheritance involved, there was a motive for foul play. Lord Peter nodded back to the inspector and clearly did not like the direction of the conversation. Holmes carried on.

"Now then, as to our findings of the immediate events leading to Miss Westbury's death, allow me to confirm that we found no evidence to prove that it was anything but a tragic accident."

The four of the St. James boys allowed their shoulders to relax and gave satisfied thin smiles. Holmes carried on.

"Of course, on the other hand, we found no evidence that would positively prove the opposite. The final conclusion I will submit is that the true and only cause of the tragic event can never be known."

"What do you mean?" said Olleitch. "There is no question at all. She went up to the roof after going for a ride, decided to water the flowers, and fell off. That was clearly established at the time. And that was the conclusion of the inquest."

"Ah, yes, Mr. Olleitch. You are entirely correct. However, you did not hire me to merely give my stamp of approval to the findings of the inquest. You requested a thorough investigation and full exoneration. Therefore, I began with the need to prove that Miss Westbury was alone on the roof all the time after she returned from her ride."

"Of course, she was," said Olleitch. "no one else was up there at all."

"No? Well now, sir, I know that the tragedy was deeply upsetting and that your time since then has been consumed with the national tour by the Chorale, and it is, therefore, possible that you have misremembered some of the events of that day. But it appears that all of you were up there as well that day. You left cigarette butts and splotches of dribbled wine all over the terrace. Miss Westbury was not a smoker."

"Oh, yes, yes," said Lord Peter. "We went up there after lunch to relax and enjoy the view, but that was hours before the accident."

"And you did not return?" asked Holmes.

"No. What reason was there to do that?"

"To have some more wine before supper and listen to the children perform their song. The four tykes did a capital rendition of *I've Been Working on the Railroad,* did they not? Of course, a child under twelve cannot be required to give sworn testimony and is protected from aggressive cross-questioning, but I fear that a judge would perceive a cloud on your account if it were to conflict with the account given by four quite adorable and exceptionally articulate children. So might also the charitable public."

Again, the look on their faces was interesting. Before they could answer, Holmes carried on.

"Please do not be overly concerned, gentlemen. There may be a small cloud on the good name of the Society, but that will go in time as long as there are no further problems arising."

The looks of assured contentment returned.

"However," said Holmes, "there is another problem that has arisen."

"And just what, Mr. Holmes is that?" demanded Lord Dalgingham. "Other than the terribly unfortunate incident regarding Miss Westbury, our Society has enjoyed a stellar reputation for probity, and scrupulous management of our mission, funds, and operations."

"Oh, indeed you have," said Holmes, "Indeed you have. With one minor exception."

"What?!" came from Olleitch.

"Well, gentlemen, it's about all that silver bullion in the basement of your house on St. James Square."

I had to hand it to them. These chaps were polished performers. The involuntary look of shock came and vanished in an instant.

"What are you talking about?" said Lord Dalgingham.

"Mr. Holmes," said Olleitch. "Haaallooo. Kindly return to planet earth. We are a Society for helping children, not a collector of silver bullion."

"Oh, dear," said Holmes. "My sincere apologies. Here I thought that you had become silver collectors. If you say I am mistaken, we can solve that problem quickly enough. Your house is no more than a ten-minute walk from where we are now. Why don't we take a break and enjoy a brisk walk over there and take a look, shall we?"

"That would be a waste of time, Mr. Holmes," said Olleitch. "The vaults in that house are secured by Chubb and cannot be opened except by an officer of the Chubb company. They are busy fellows, and we make those arrangements several days in advance, so kindly move on with your report."

"Ah, yes, time is of the essence. How inconsiderate of me to forget. Perhaps we can just send one of our constables here to take a look and report back."

"Mr. Holmes, what are you saying? He cannot look in our vaults without opening them, and it cannot be opened without the combination, and only an officer of Chubb has that information."

Holmes turned in his chair and addressed one of the police officers.

"Officer Mallowford, as you already have your notebook and pencil at the ready, kindly jot down these numbers. 44, 15, 58, 22. That is the combination for the vault on the left side of the stairs. I do not have the one on the right side stored in my memory, but a look into one of the vaults should be sufficient, I would assume."

He now smiled back at the five men who were not smiling in return.

"That will not be necessary, Mr. Holmes. As it is fully within our responsibility as trustees, we have been setting aside a portion of the income of the Society as a prudent measure. We have chosen to invest in silver and other forms of securities as they are known to deliver a much better rate of return than merely putting the money into a bank account."

"Oh, why yes, of course. If that is what you have been doing, then it is a clear indication of your astute and responsible management of the funds entrusted to you. Allow me to compliment you on your perspicacity."

"Thank you," said Dalgingham. "Please move on to the next item in your report."

"I would wish to do that, sir, but unfortunately, there is another problem."

"What now?" said Olleitch, rolling his eyes.

"It concerns," said Holmes, "the value of the silver you have set aside as a reserve. According to my investigation, it is now well over one million pounds. Isn't that somewhat excessive of the amount necessary?"

"Don't be absurd," said Olleitch. "It is nowhere near that much."

"You don't say," said Holmes. "Very well now, I must have made a mistake in calculating my sums. You see, I have here a file showing the transactions of your Society with …"

Holmes proceeded to read off the record of the purchases made from silver mining firms throughout the world, the debits to the bank account of the Society, the delivery confirmations to the building on St. James Square, and his computation of the value based on the price of ounces of silver on the days of the delivery. He looked up at the faces glaring back at him.

"Oh dear, I appear to have upset you. Please, gentlemen, I am have only done what you hired me to do. I am loath to blow my own horn, but when you ask Sherlock Holmes to carry out an investigation, I have to defend my reputation and do it thoroughly and properly. Is that not right, Inspector Lestrade?"

Another sideways look from Lestrade. "Right, Holmes."

Olleitch exploded. "The records of our accounts are private and confidential! How dare you or anyone invade our privacy like that!"

Before Holmes could reply, the answer came in a bellow from the armchair in the corner of the room.

"DON'T BE STUPID!" said Mycroft Holmes, somewhat more loudly than was necessary. "You know bloody well that Her Majesty's government can inspect the accounts and transactions of anyone who does business anywhere in the Empire."

Mycroft had opened his eyes and leaned forward in his chair whilst thus pontificating. He now closed them again and slumped back.

"Mr. Holmes," said Dalgingham, "you are clearly not a man of business and commerce, and you appear to unaware that the value of silver has increased substantially over this past year. As men who have confidential access to the events that transpire in The City, I can assure you that anyone who knows anything about the value of precious metals will tell you that the value of silver is expected to continue to rise quickly until at least the end of the first quarter of 1897. The intent of the directors—and I trust you will consider this information privileged and confidential—is to retain the silver until that time and only then sell it at four or five times the cost of purchase. We shall then be in the position to use those funds to help many more destitute children in Calcutta than we could have had we sent the funds overseas immediately upon receiving them from England's charitable public. I trust you will acknowledge the wisdom in our plan. And I would also expect that you would keep your mouth closed concerning it."

A look of astonishment—feigned, I assure you—appeared on the countenance of Sherlock Holmes.

"Why … why, yes. How brilliant. How very brilliant. Very well then, I have no problem at all with your sagacity and acuity."

"Good," said Olleitch. "I should hope not."

"Well, not all that good. You see, while I might not have a problem with your management of the Society, I fear the Commissioner of Charities does. He considers himself the trustee of trustees, and he has some strong opinions on your practices."

"You informed him?" said Dalgingham.

"Well, of course, I did, Your Lordship. To fulfill my responsibility to do a full report for you, I had to avail myself of all the laws and regulations pertaining to charitable trusts. Therefore, I requested an audience with the Commissioner. He informed me that he has no quarrel with a charity's setting aside a reasonable portion of its annual income as a reserve to guard against unexpected declines in income in the future. However, he told me to tell you that his yardstick is that a society such as yours is entitled to spend twenty percent of its income on its own operations and to set aside ten percent as a reserve during each fiscal year. The remaining seventy percent must be disbursed to the stated recipients as designated in your charter. His problem is that for the past three years, your Society has been setting aside seventy percent and only disbursing ten percent. And that just will not do."

"So, he is not happy with us," said Olleitch. "there's nothing he can do about it short of taking away our charter, and that would be fought in court for years."

"I regret to inform you," said Holmes, "that he can seize your silver bullion and sell it on the market and then disburse the funds to your homes in Calcutta."

"How dare he. He cannot do that!" said Dalgingham.

Again, a response came from the armchair in the corner.

"Don't be an imbecile. He can, and he will."

Mycroft returned to his position of sloping from the headrest to the floor.

The directors were exchanging glances and whispers and not looking at all at ease with what they had just been told. Holmes spoke to them in a gentle, comforting voice.

"Gentlemen, gentlemen. There is no need to be overly concerned. There is a perfectly good solution to this problem. There are still ten business days left in the year. That is more than enough time for you to put ninety percent of your silver holdings up for auction at the London Metals Exchange and then to disburse the funds to your affiliated homes in Calcutta. All you have to do is inform them that they will be receiving their entire income for the year 1897 all at once and to make sure that they budget accordingly for the rest of the year."

Dalgingham looked at him, somewhat askance. "And that would be acceptable?"

"I believe it would. Do you agree, Inspector Lestrade?"

"Right, Holmes."

"Then that," said Dalgingham, "is what we shall do. Now then, Mr. Holmes, is there anything else in your report?"

"No, that is it for my written report. But there is one other item."

"What now?"

"As trustees and directors, indeed as gentlemen, you really should not be hiring thugs to beat up young students. It's just not done."

"What are you talking about?"

"There are four chaps over in Spitalfields who go by the names of Tommy Todgers, Freddie Deeming, Ikey Solomon and Christopher Theakstone. They told an inspector from Scotland Yard, informally of course, that a Mr. Timothy Olleitch hired them to give a beating to a young man from Cambridge. Really, such actions just are not the thing to do if you are to retain your sterling image in front of the public. Now, good day, gentlemen. I will not be submitting an invoice for my services. In consideration of the wonderful work of the charity, it has been my pleasure to carry out the work *pro bono*."

The five men shuffled out of the room and walked in silence down the hall to the door of the club. I could only imagine the conversation that would emerge as soon as they stepped on to the pavement of Pall Mall.

Left standing in the Strangers' Room were Lestrade, Holmes, and me, and left reclining was Mycroft Holmes. Lestrade, somewhat angrily, challenged Holmes.

"Just what, Holmes, was the meaning of that? You brought me into this case because you suspected those men of murder. And now you have sent them off with the means of getting away scot-free. Have you lost your mind?"

"No, my dear Inspector. I assure you, there is method in my madness. We do not have sufficient evidence to identify the most likely subjects in the murder of Miss Westbury, let alone gain a conviction in a court of law. And being able to lay a charge for a murder they orchestrated in Calcutta is beyond praying. Would you agree, Inspector?

Yet another sideways look. "Right, Holmes. Go on."

"Our only hope for putting them away for a decade or more is to convict them of fraud, the illegal absconding with of massive amounts of money. I am reasonably confident that they are now about to do just that and that they are facing a deadline to get it started."

"You think they are going to find some way to sell the silver and send the funds to India and somehow manage to get them sent back and end up in their pockets. Is that it?"

"Precisely. They do not know, nor even suspect, that we can observe not only the movement of money in and out of bank accounts in England, but that we also have the ability to watch what happens to every farthing after the funds arrive in India. The only blank link in the chain is the movement through Switzerland."

"Right, those Swiss banks are a dark, mysterious hole if ever there was one. Nobody can tell what goes on inside them."

"Exactly. It is impossible."

A sharp reply came from the armchair.

"Don't be morons. Both of you. Of course, we can find out what happens in Switzerland."

Lestrade looked puzzled.

"How can we do that?" he demanded of Mycroft Holmes. "The Swiss are supposed to be the best in the world at keeping secrets."

"Good Lord, Inspector, they are not only Swiss, they are bankers. They keep the secrets of those who pay them to do so. If we offer them more to reveal what they are keeping secret, they spill the beans. And as long as we keep winning the bid, they then keep our secret."

"Oh … indeed," said Lestrade. "And here I thought …"

He departed, shaking his head.

Chapter Twenty-Three

The Money Moves

The following day, Monday, the twenty-first of December, a notice appeared in *The Financial Times* announcing an auction of silver bullion. It would be managed by Christie's and would begin on 23 December, pause over Christmas and Boxing Day, and continue on the twenty-eighth until all of the blocks put up for auction had been sold.

The identity of the seller and the overall amount of bullion that would be available for purchase was not revealed. As expected, the first lots to appear went for an astronomical price. As the days wore on, the price fell as the buyers became aware that a massive amount was still to be sold. By 30 January, the reserve bid had been dropped to the market price as it had been in October. By the end of that day, the last lot was auctioned off.

The proceeds from the auction were in excess of seven hundred and fifty thousand pounds. Such an event might have been news had it not happened over Christmas. As it was, even the lords of the City were not paying attention, and the gossip and speculation were confined to the fraternity of silversmiths.

On the morning of the first day of 1897, Mr. Marvin Bethune dropped into 221B Baker Street.

"I thought you might like to know, Mr. Holmes," he said, "that before the stroke of midnight last night, over six hundred and seventy-five thousand pounds was wired from the Bank of England to the Bank of Calcutta."

"That amount," said Holmes, "is seventy-five thousand pounds short of the total."

"Aye, 'tis. Christie's took their commission. It did wonders for their end-of-the-year accounts. They were very eager to hold another auction as soon as possible."

"And the Bank of England?"

"Aye, they took their bit as well, as did the Bank of Calcutta, but there will be an enormous amount still to be given to the children and the homes."

"That, sir, I sincerely doubt. I expect that they shall receive a generous transfer but that some way will be found to direct much if not most of it back to England. We shall not have to wait long. A week or two at the most."

Holmes was wrong.

During the first half of January, funds were paid out from the Bank of Calcutta to the ten affiliated children's homes, but an entire month passed, and we saw not a farthing transferred into the accounts of the five men with whom we had met. I began to question whether we might be dealing with honest men after all.

"Please, Watson," said Holmes. "They are not honest, but neither are they foolish. They are, I will allow, more clever than I gave them credit for. Perhaps their time on the rugby pitch taught them the discipline needed to defer their reward until the most advantageous time."

On the eighteenth of February, all of the newspapers devoted numerous headlines and pages of print to the triumphant British expedition to Benin. The little city-state had been torched, and its treasures and wealth had been looted and was on its way back to London. On that same day, five hundred pounds was sent from

Calcutta through Zurich. One hundred pounds arrived in each of the accounts of the directors.

"It was another test," said Holmes. "Just a ripple so as not to attract attention. The tidal wave is coming."

At the end of February, the children who had constituted the Chorale of Angels departed England and returned to Calcutta.

Another test took place in mid-March. These deposits were more difficult to follow as each of the directors had opened multiple bank accounts in several banks and cities of England. However, it is impossible to stay hidden from the tentacles of the Exchequer.

"A man has a choice," said Holmes. "Either he can send his money through reliable channels and know that it will arrive safely. Or he can find a way of doing so that is beyond the global reach of the Bank of England and the agents of Her Majesty's government. He cannot do both."

In April, a package was delivered to Baker Street that had been sent from Calcutta. Inside were packages of tea, silk gloves, and small bottles of fine Indian spices. They were sent by Misses Yamini and Arunima along with their repeated apologies for whatever distress their story had caused Sherlock Holmes.

"Were they, "I asked Holmes, "referring to the story about your reprehensible harassment of young women or to your marriage to Irene Adler?"

"That will do, Watson."

Throughout the winter and into the spring, Holmes had his Irregulars follow the five men who controlled the Society and report back to him. For day after day, they informed Holmes that they had seen nothing untoward, and it was clear to me if not to Holmes that they were on the verge of resigning their positions due to utter boredom. Holmes was forced to increase their wages by several shillings.

Then, on a Monday in late March, something did happen. Each of the five men was followed to a branch bank on the edge of the city, and they were seen sitting with the local manager and opening an account. The following day, each of them went to another bank and opened a second account. A third account was opened the next day.

Each of the five men opened their three accounts, all within a radius of a mile or two of each other.

Holmes forwarded the data to Mr. Bethune and Inspector Lestrade.

Nothing happened in April.

And nothing happened in May, except for a visit to 221B by Miss Violet Westbury, her mother, and aging grandfather.

"Mr. Holmes," said Miss Westbury, "I cannot understand why the delay. When my fiancé was murdered, you were able to solve the mystery and have the villains arrested within a few days. It is now eight months since Isabella died, and nothing has happened. Those men have gotten away with murder. What are you doing?"

"I assure you, Miss Westbury, that the murder of Mr. Cadogan West, while ingenious in its villainy, required no more than a few hours of logical deduction to solve. After doing so, the culprits were easily identified, and the case to be presented in court was straightforward. Your sister's death does not lend itself to such a direct solution. I cannot prove that her death was not accidental, nor which of the possible suspects were involved, or even if all of them were. Therefore, I must be patient. I must give them enough rope and allow them to hang themselves. I fully understand your distress and can only ask that you be patient."

Patience, as they say, is a virtue seldom found in women, and never found in a young woman whose beloved sister has been murdered.

By June, I had almost forgotten about the case. Sherlock Holmes had not. Neither had Violet Westbury. On the fifteenth of June, she again paid a visit to Baker Street and demanded that Holmes take more action on the case.

"How can you just let this go on, Mr. Holmes? How can you? Those men are enjoying every minute of their lives while my sister has had hers taken away from her. You have to do something."

"I expect," he said, "for a significant development to take place around 20, 21, and 22 of June."

I was puzzled. "What," I asked, "has the summer solstice to do with the case?"

"No, my dear Watson, it has nothing to do with the solstice. It has everything to do with the Diamond Jubilee of our beloved Queen Victoria."

"But nothing will be happening on those days. The entire nation will be consumed with celebrating."

"Precisely."

On the twenty-first of June, around nine o'clock in the evening, Mr. Marvin Bethune arrived at 221B, quite breathless from his racing up the stairs.

"They did it," he said. "They did it."

"They did what?" I asked.

"They transferred the money. Three days ago, the Bank of Calcutta received large deposits from the ten children's homes with instructions to wire the funds to the bank in Zurich. Yesterday, over twenty-five smaller transfers were sent to those new accounts at the banks around London. Over five hundred thousand pounds in total was sent and received."

"Tomorrow," said Holmes, "while the country is consumed by the Jubilee, I expect they will withdraw the money. We shall be waiting for them."

On the twenty-second of June, when all the families of London lined the route of the Queen's Jubilee procession, and all offices and banks were emptied except for a skeleton staff, the five men made their move.

A team of officers from Scotland Yard, under the supervision of Inspectors Linseed and Mallowford, surreptitiously followed them. During the morning hours, the men paid a visit to their three banks and withdrew the funds from their accounts.

From there, they made their way to a pub amidst the throngs of citizens who were gathered near Westminster Abbey. They sat there and talked for half-an-hour. The officers who were observing them, obscured by the crowds, had the impression that there was some conflict amongst them.

At three o'clock, two of them, Timothy Olleitch and Lord Peter Dalgingham, took a cab to Waterloo and boarded the train for Dover. Decimus Fernsby and Baron Montague Fitz Leigh went the other direction and traveled to Victoria. There they caught the train to Southampton. Oliver Glasshover walked back to the house on St. James Square.

Early in the evening, Olleitch and Dalgingham were quietly arrested by Scotland Yard as they were about to board the ferry to Calais. At around the same hour, Fernsby and Fitz Leigh were stopped and taken into custody before boarding the *S.S. Auguste Victoria*, a Hamburg Line ship about to sail for New York. Oliver Glasshover answered the door at the private clubhouse on St. James Square and was led to a waiting police wagon.

All five of the men had in their possession a valise containing the equivalent in British and American paper currency of one-hundred thousand pounds.

Throughout the evening, Holmes, Lestrade, Mycroft Holmes, and I sat in the Strangers' Room. Telegrams and notes from the arresting officers were sent in every few minutes. It would have been more efficient had we gathered at Scotland Yard, but there was no possibility of having Mycroft Holmes lower his habits to such a mundane level.

Once it had been confirmed to us that all five men and their money were in custody, Lestrade posed the next immediate question.

"Arresting those blighters will be front-page news in every paper for a week. I will send a note out to the Press and have them come together tomorrow morning for the announcement."

"No, you will not," said Mycroft Holmes.

Lestrade was visibly upset by that remark and demanded an explanation.

"Such stories," said Mycroft, "would reflect badly on *all* charities, and we do not want to destroy the confidence the public has in them."

"Ah, yes," said Sherlock Holmes. "The rest of them—and there are scores more forming every year—do fine work on behalf of so many good causes."

"Don't be ridiculous," said Mycroft. "Their good works are irrelevant in comparison to the beneficial effects of enlightened public policy. No, no. We have to keep the charities looking good for a much better reason. If they were to vanish, then members of the Royal Family would have nothing whatsoever left to do to justify their existence. The demands for a republic would become irresistible."

"Then what," I asked, "will you do?"

"We shall," said Mycroft, "follow the much more discreet course. We shall take their money away from them and have it held in trust by the Commissioner of Charities, and then a small announcement will be posted stating that the current board of directors has retired, their terms having been completed, and a new set will take over. That's what the banks and insurance firms do whenever they are caught with fingers in the till. It will do for a philanthropic society just as well."

That was, indeed, what happened. The five men were charged with numerous violations of law relating to theft and fraud and kept in custody in HMP Pentonville. On the third day of their incarceration, a note arrived for Holmes. It was from Mr. Oliver Glasshover requesting a private meeting with him. On Monday, 28 June 1897, that meeting took place in the visitors' meeting room of the prison.

Chapter Twenty-Four

One of Them Confesses

"Are you prepared," asked Holmes of Glasshover, "to make a full confession? The courts will treat you more lightly if you do."

"No, but I am prepared to confess to two matters."

"I am all attention, sir. Proceed."

"The first to the stupidity of arrogance that led us to think it was a clever idea to invite the famous Mr. Sherlock Holmes to carry out an investigation. That was not a good idea."

"I could have told you that," said Holmes. "The second?"

"I confess to being absolutely certain that Mr. Sherlock Holmes is far more interested in what happened to cause the death of Miss Isabella Westbury than he is in making sure some so-called orphans in Calcutta receive enough support for their daily bowl of rice. Am I correct, Mr. Holmes?"

They gave each other hard looks for several seconds before Holmes nodded ever so slightly.

"That is correct. Carry on."

"I am fully aware that you do not have the authority of a Crown Prosecutor to negotiate a change in the charges, but I am also quite certain that you are willing to exchange favors between Englishmen for whom, regardless of our faults, our word is our bond."

"I am willing. Should you provide me with data that leads to knowing the truth about Miss Westbury, I will use whatever influence I might have to encourage the police, Crown, and judge to treat you accordingly. On that, you have my word. Now then, what can you tell me about her death?"

"To start with, you should know that I was rather fond of her. I met her at the first directors' meeting she attended last autumn, and we were beginning to enjoy a romantic friendship. I had intended to ask her to marry me."

"Which," said Holmes, "she quite likely would have turned down as she had several other proposals over the past two years from men who were a decade closer to her age than you are."

Judging by the look on his face, Glasshover didn't like that comment. Holmes, on the other hand, had no time for attempts to manipulate his judgment with emotional prefaces before the story began.

"That may be true, Mr. Holmes. However, I would have also offered her the opportunity to join an exclusive group of remarkable individuals who are destined to play a leading role in the transformation of the world into a far superior place than it is now."

"You are referring," said Holmes, "to the exclusive and elusive Order of the Fittest, five of whose members are now in prison for robbing orphans. That exclusive group? Kindly get on with what you know about her death."

Anger flickered in Glasshover's eyes, but he quickly recovered his composure and replied.

"Very well then, yes, about her death. During a meeting earlier that day, she had asked to see the records of the transfers of funds through to the children's homes in Calcutta. Her request was obstructed by our General Secretary, Mr. Olleitch. However, his excuses for not being able to provide the information were all parried by Miss Isabella, and her demands became quite insistent. When we adjourned briefly for a refreshment break, I asked her, in the friendly tone of one who cared for her, why she was so upset over the matter.

She confided in me a secret that, with her death, is now known only to me."

"You are referring, no doubt, to her direct correspondence with the managers of the homes in which they disclosed the maintenance fees paid through the Swiss consulate in Calcutta."

Mr. Glasshover was shocked by Holmes's reply and did not remove the look of stunned surprise from his face for several long seconds.

"I see that Sherlock Holmes has been doing his homework."

"It is what you and the other directors of the Society hired me to do, was it not? Return to your story. Start when the tea break has ended."

"If I may, sir, I shall resume during the tea break. I noticed that Peter and Timothy had taken Miss Isabella aside and were having some words with her. I could not hear what they were saying, but it was apparent that there was some animosity between them. After returning to the meeting table, Peter, as the chairman of the meeting, announced that we were moving on to the next item on the agenda. Miss Isabella raised an objection, and there was vigorous debate. I took the side of the young lady and championed her position as I believed that she was in the right."

"Did you?" asked Holmes. "Or were you attempting to advance your romantic intentions toward her by appearing to support her position."

"My motives may have been mixed. Nevertheless, the meeting moved on, and we covered the topics for the day. Immediately after, Peter and Isabella could be heard as they stood together on the staircase arguing with each other. But then we all moved up to the roof terrace for afternoon refreshments and to listen to the four children perform their song. When they were finished, Peter came to me and asked if I would mind taking the four of them down to the kitchen and organizing a treat of peaches and cream. I did so and remained in the kitchen with them and the cook for the next ten minutes."

"Stop there," said Holmes. "Can you confirm that during that time, the other four men were still on the roof with Miss Isabella?"

"When I departed from the roof, they were there. It was not until ten minutes had passed whilst I was in the kitchen with the children that I heard hurried footsteps descending the staircase. However, there was no talking, and I could not tell how many there were. It sounded as if they all made their way into the library. It was then that the cry went up from the maid. She had gone outside after hearing a scream, and she found Miss Isabella. All of the men rushed out from the library and acted as if they were horribly shocked and stricken with grief upon seeing her dead."

"And do you believe," said Holmes, "that those four men colluded to murder her by throwing her over the balustrade to her death? Is that what you are telling me?"

"Yes, and I assure you that my shock and grief were sincere even if theirs were not."

"Of course. Now, kindly defend your accusation."

"They all stuck by the same story of leaving her on the terrace while they descended to the library for another round of drinks before supper. But there were discrepancies in their accounts. One said that Isabella had already begun to water the flower baskets before they left her. Another said that she was still sipping on a cup of tea. A third said that he saw her pick up the watering can."

"That is a reason," said Holmes, "to believe that they colluded in the murder, but it does not identify those who carried it out."

"I believe it was all four of them."

"Why?"

"All four were wounded. Isabella must have put up quite the fight. Decimus was bleeding from his wrist and sought to have it bathed and bound up soon after. Montague had scratches on his face. Timothy was dapping a handkerchief to his left eye, and Peter was walking with a distinct limp, as if he had a sharp pain in the groin. I am aware that that is not sufficient evidence to stand up in court, but it is what I saw, and that is my conclusion."

"Why did you not tell this to the police or to me earlier than today?"

"For the sake, Mr. Holmes, of a quarter-million pounds."

Holmes's eyes widened, and I took in a sharp gasp.

"Explain," said Holmes.

"The plan was already in place whereby we would have most of the money we sent to the homes in Calcutta routed back to us through Switzerland. It would be sent in a series of many small transfers and directed to a score of bank accounts in and around London. By Christmas of this current year, each of us would have gained over two-hundred and fifty thousand pounds."

"Which would have been jeopardized if you had gone to the police with your suspicions."

"Correct, Mr. Holmes. Your report to us forced us to move prematurely. We should have suspected that we had been set up by Sherlock Holmes."

"But now you are breaking ranks with your colleagues. Why are you doing so?"

"I have been friends with them since our school days at Harrow. In the past few years, they have developed some beliefs that I cannot go along with."

"Beliefs," said Holmes, "related to the superiority of the British race to all other lesser forms of life on earth, and the need to improve the bloodlines of the general populace by selective breeding and legal enforcement of eugenics? Those beliefs?"

"Yes, among others."

"But you kept up your close connection to them as long as there was a prospect of becoming very rich through the charity scheme."

"Yes, I did."

"But with the vanishing of that reward, you now wish to break free of them and assist in their prosecution. Your enlightened conversion is terribly convenient."

"You may see it that way, Mr. Holmes. I would add that I felt deep anger and grief over what happened to Isabella."

"The value of which fell well short of a quarter-million pounds."

"I am not arguing with you, sir. I am only informing you of my current beliefs and actions. I expect that you will now keep your word, regardless of whatever low opinion you have of me."

"I will do that, and I trust that your time in prison will be useful to the improvement of your character. I expect to see you next in court. Good day, sir."

Once Holmes and I were out on the pavement in front of Pentonville, I asked his opinion.

"Do you," I said, "believe his story?"

"His presence in the kitchen at the time Miss Isabella was falling can be easily confirmed by the staff. I shall have Baynes check into that. His infatuation with a lovely young woman was indicated by her family. I assume that the director they said took a fancy to her was Mr. Glasshover. If confirmed, then it is probable he is telling the truth even if he is somewhat despicable as a human being."

"Are you going to help him?"

"I will tell the Westbury family what he has said and that I am inclined to believe him. They are my clients, and I have a duty to keep them informed. When the case comes to court, I shall fulfill my part of the agreement. Until then, I shall do whatever I can to make sure all five of them stay in prison. Their schemes are devious and dangerous, and it is better that they are not released back to the streets of London."

Unfortunately, Holmes underestimated their abilities.

Chapter Twenty-Five

The Battle in Court

The summer of 1897 was relatively uneventful in England. Like all summers on our sceptered isle, it was unhappily shorter and less sunny than the populace had hoped for.

Events in other parts of the world filled the front pages of our newspapers. The American chap, Mark Twain, reported on the exaggerated reports of his death. News of finding over a ton of gold in the Klondike area of the Yukon started a stampede, a gold rush, of men from across America and even from England and Europe who booked passage to Alaska in the hope of having a fortune wash into their saucepans.

There was a terrible earthquake in Assam that left over a thousand dead and buildings destroyed or damaged all the way from Calcutta to Delhi. A notice from the Society for the Care of Street Orphans appeared immediately in the newspapers calling upon the good people of the Empire to make a special generous contribution to help repair the heart-breaking damage to the children's homes. I could not, for the life of me, discern who had placed the notice, what with the directors and general secretary being in jail.

Other than that, I had more or less forgotten about the case and had turned my attention to writing about some of the more recent cases that had been presented to and subsequently solved by Sherlock Holmes.

Holmes, however, busy though he was, had not forgotten. Throughout July and August, he worked diligently in cooperation with Scotland Yard and the Crown Prosecutor to assemble a damning case against the miscreants who had so deviously manipulated the good intentions of the British people and robbed from the poorest of the poor. He also paid fortnightly visits to the Westbury home in Chelsea and kept the bereaved family abreast of any developments in the case.

The trial was scheduled to start on Monday, 13 September. I had assumed that it would be held in the Old Bailey, but Holmes informed me otherwise.

"The trial," said Holmes, "will be held in one of the lower courts that handles property crimes. There is insufficient evidence to bring a charge of murder or even criminal negligence leading to death. Therefore, we will pursue the strongest case of theft and fraud and vigorously advocate for a sentence of ten years."

Only a few members of the Press attended the trial, and they vanished after the second day when the news arrived about twenty striking miners being killed by local police In Pennsylvania. Reporters immediately focused their efforts on interviewing Americans who happened to be in London and asking them how they felt about the news. The only occupants of chairs in the public gallery were Mr. Harris Paterson, Mrs. Westbury, and Miss Violet Westbury.

The Crown Prosecutor did a workmanlike job of presenting the evidence in a systematic and logical way. Documents from banks in London and Calcutta were presented that proved, beyond a shadow of a doubt, that the officers of the charitable trust had not only abrogated their fiduciary responsibility but had committed a brazen theft of an enormous sum of money intended for the care of orphans. Three senior men from the Bank of England attested to the veracity of the documents and insisted that the Old Lady of Threadneedle Street had acted with complete integrity and was in no way complicit in the fraud.

Holmes had managed to find a missionary who had served for years under the London Mission to India. Mr. Jonathan Norris Groves, with some reluctance and moving modesty, confirmed that the book,

Three Cups of Rice, was considered by old India hands to be a work of fiction, written to advance the reputation of the authors at the expense of the children of India.

With a handful of minor exceptions, the barrister acting for the defense did not exercise his right to cross-question and generally ignored everything that had been said by the witnesses.

By the time the case for the prosecution had been completed, the jury were all looking daggers at Dalgingham, Olleitch and company. I felt quite assured that a verdict of guilty on all charges would be delivered, and a severe sentence imposed. Holmes and the Crown were similarly inclined.

We were wrong. We vastly underestimated the audacity of the defendants.

Their barrister began by producing a stack of affidavits, all attesting to the probity and sterling character of the defendants. The signatories were an impressive list of men, including but not limited to bishops, nobility of all ranks and riches, members of parliament, captains of industry and commerce, doctors, professors, and poets and writers who ranged from creators of sensationalist penny dreadfuls to the current poet laureate of Great Britain.

All had submitted in writing their willingness to appear before the court and testify under oath to their belief that the officers and directors of the Society had led lives of unwavering commitment to philanthropy and had not a single blemish ever written against their names. Four of them were called upon to confirm their assertions from the witness box, which they did with considerable verve and forcefulness.

Mycroft had advised our barrister that the four of them were all active members of the mysterious house on St. James Square, but when challenged on this connection to the defendants, all of them had a ready answer.

"My good man," said Viscount Quentin-Whimby when cross-questioned, "I am a member only of White's, and I have friends in almost every first-rank club in London. I visit often with them at their clubs. Of course, I know these gentlemen and have been their guests as they have been mine."

The non-existence of a list of members of the said house made it impossible to contradict their claims.

Next came a Mr. Sekh Sahonawez, who was confirmed to be a laborer in Limehouse. He testified that he had himself been an orphan on the streets of Calcutta and had been destined to a life of crime and grinding poverty. At the tender age of twelve, he had been rescued by workers from the Jewels for Jesus home and, by the grace of God, had been able to learn a trade, find gainful employment, and, with the assistance of one of the directors, had emigrated to England.

Our barrister attempted to expose contradictions and gaps in his story but to no avail.

"He has been," muttered Holmes when the witness stood down, "expertly coached and rehearsed."

Then came the *pièce de résistance*.

A Mr. Mohes Chunder Chuckerbutty, who had arrived in England from India only one day ago, was called to the stand. He identified himself as the director of the His Precious Lambs Home for Children in the Parnasree Palli neighborhood of Calcutta. It was one of the ten homes that had received the enormous subvention from the Society. As the barrister for the defense led him with finely worded questions, he asserted that the idea of returning most of the money had originated with the directors of the homes.

"We cannot trust our own banks, sir," he testified. "They are very corrupt. Very, very corrupt indeed, sir. We all knew that if we left that much money in our accounts, it would disappear as quickly as does the cobra when the mongoose appears. We met and agreed that we must send most of the money back to the Society for safe-keeping and have it doled out to us in equal portions over the next three years. We did that, sir, because we trust the banks in England, but no Indian banker can be trusted with access to that much money. So, we insisted that the Society receive most of the money back. We sent the money through the Swiss consulate because they have very much lower rates for such services than the Bank of England does, and we trust the Swiss as well even if they are the best in the world at keeping secrets. And that is what happened, sir. You may ask the directors of the other homes, and they will all agree with what I have said, so help me God."

We had not seen that one coming. Our adversaries delivered a left hook out of nowhere, and we had nothing prepared with which to respond.

Our barristers strove valiantly to pick apart Mr. Chuckerbutty's story. When did the ten directors meet? Where? Who first broached the idea? Who was the contact at the Swiss Consulate and at *Debit Suisse*? Who agreed on how much to send back to England?

For all these questions, credible answers were given. When asked why the transfers to England were distributed amongst twenty smaller bank branches, the man professed apparent ignorance and could only suggest that it was the way the Swiss chose to do business so as not to attract attention. Any Englishman who has ever been to Switzerland would have to agree with his conjecture.

The trial ended on that note. The Crown tried to diminish the account of the chap from Calcutta by reminding the jury that all five men had removed the funds in cash from their multiple accounts and that four of them were apprehended attempting to flee the country. These were not the actions, he insisted, of men who had no intention of returning the money to the starving orphans of Calcutta.

The barrister for the defense returned again and again to the character witnesses who had stated under oath that the accused had never and could never commit such a crime. He concluded by repeating the startling testimony of the man from Calcutta who, we had to admit, seemed highly credible even if we did not believe a word of what he said.

The jury deliberated for two hours and returned to the courtroom. Several of them looked over at the row of defendants and nodded. That was not a good sign.

The foreman announced the decisions that had been reached and declared that the defendants had been found not guilty on every one of the serious charges. The only charge which they agreed had been substantiated was the operating of a boarding house for children without having obtained the proper license.

The judge thanked the jury and pronounced the sentence. It seemed to me that he had not been fooled by the false testimony but had no choice but the honor the decision of the jury, and he refused to allow the five hundred thousand pounds of cash that had been found in the possession of the defendants to be returned to them. It would continue to be held in trust by the Commissioner of Charities and was to be sent out in installments to the various children's homes at the discretion of the Commissioner. Annual audited statements, carried out by registered Indian accountants, would be required before the subvention for the next year would be sent.

As to prison time, he had little choice but to agree that the time already served was more than sufficient punishment of the sole misdemeanor of which they had been found guilty.

The judge banged his gavel on the bench and declared the trial over. The defendants all rose to their feet, smiling and giving each other pats on the back. The shook hands with their barrister and waved to the departing jury as they all filed out of the courtroom.

On our side of the aisle, no one moved. Neither did the three people who were sitting in the public gallery.

I felt as if my chest had descended into my gut. We might have succeeded in removing from those men their ill-gotten gains, but they had, I was sure, gotten away with murder.

Holmes slowly rose and walked back to speak to the family. Before he could say a word, Miss Violet Westbury expressed her profound disappointment.

"Mr. Holmes, we have waited a year for justice to be done. We put all our hopes in you, and now the men who murdered my sister have walked away. Are you going to do anything?"

"I assure you," Holmes replied, "that I shall not rest until they receive the punishment due to them. All I ask of you is that you continue to be patient."

"I fear," said Miss Violet, "that our patience has run out. We shall no longer require your services and shall proceed without you from now on."

"Perfectly understandable," said Holmes. "However, I shall continue on my own. Please accept my apologies and best wishes."

The family made their egress from the courtroom, and we followed them out to the pavement. The defendants and their barristers were gathered there, enjoying a cigarette and chatting jovially about their victory. Lord Dalgingham stepped away from the gaggle and approached Holmes, smiling broadly.

"I say there, old sport," he said, "You chaps put up a jolly good game in there. But, just like on the pitch, you win some, you lose some. Be assured, no hard feelings, I hope, eh, Mr. Holmes?"

"Peter Dalgingham," said Holmes, "you are a thief and a murderer, and I shall not rest until I see you hanged by the neck until you are dead. Let me assure you that every night as you go to bed and every morning when you wake up, I am coming for you, and I am bringing Hell with me."

Holmes turned and walked away. The smile vanished from the face of His Lordship.

Chapter Twenty-Six

A Crazed Lumberjack?

Inspector Lestrade and I hurried to catch up with Holmes as he marched away from the courthouse. Lestrade grabbed him by the arm and forced him to stop.

"Holmes," he said, pointing his finger at the sternum of the man he was speaking to. "You know, and I know that what took place in there was a travesty, a gross miscarriage of justice. But don't you dare try and take justice into your own hands. We will watch those villains, and someday we will catch them and give them the punishment they deserve. You keep your fingers out of it."

For a minute, Holmes did not answer. He looked at the inspector and then looked up to the sky and then replied.

"I give you my word, my good Inspector, that I will most certainly pursue the course of justice, but I promise you I shall not commit any serious felony whilst doing so. That is the best I can say."

"Very well, Holmes. I've watched you long enough to know that you can act like a cool, calculating machine on the outside, but that inside you are seething. Right? So, do not do anything foolish."

Holmes's face softened. "It is a good thing that we have come to know each other so well, Inspector. Acting together, we have a far better chance of success. I will also promise to keep you informed. Good day, Inspector."

Lestrade walked back to the waiting police carriage. Now I took Holmes by the arm and held him.

"Now, look here, Holmes. You cannot go off half-cocked on a path of revenge. Just what are you planning?"

"Planning? Nothing yet. I am merely making a list in my mind of all of the potential actions I might take that fall just short of committing a felony. Would you like to know them?"

"No."

For the next few days, I saw nothing of Holmes. I kept myself busy with my writing and my surgery and assumed that sometime over the coming months, he would lay out a trap for the villains of the still-prospering Society. I did not have to wait anywhere near that long.

In the early morning of Monday, 20 September, Holmes and I were seated at the breakfast table, enjoying yet another of Mrs. Hudson's meals. I had not slept well and had spent much of the night up and reading. It upset me that an entire year had passed since the tragic death of Miss Isabella Westbury, and I wondered how much longer I would have to wait for Sherlock Holmes to finally triumph and bring the villains to justice.

Not long, it turned out.

As we were finishing our morning tea, we heard a carriage pull up outside the door on Baker Street. An urgent banging at the door immediately followed, and I hustled downstairs to respond. A uniformed police officer rushed past me and up the stairs.

"Pardon me, Dr. Watson," he said as he leapt past three steps with each bound. "We need you and Mr. Holmes to come at once."

By the time I had made my way back up to our floor, Holmes was already pulling on his overcoat, and I did likewise.

"Please, Constable," said Holmes, "can you tell me where you are taking us?"

"St. James Square. Inspector Lestrade sent for you and told us to get you there immediately."

The streets were not yet crowded, and the driver of the police carriage whipped the horses in a gallop.

"Any idea," I asked Holmes as we bounced along, "what this is all about?"

"None whatsoever."

The carriage stopped in front of the clubhouse we had visited in the dark some months ago. Two more police carriages were parked in front of it, and a dozen or more uniformed constables had been posted around it, cordoning off the perimeter.

"This way, please, gentlemen," the constable who had fetched us said. "Inspector Lestrade is inside."

As we followed him onto the house, I glanced into the front parlor. Seated in one of the armchairs, clad in his housecoat and looking ghastly pale was Mr. Oliver Glasshover. A constable was standing guard over him. Holmes and I both stopped momentarily but were urged on toward the back staircase.

"Inspector Lestrade," said the same constable, "is on the second floor. Follow me, please."

As we walked through the house, we passed the library. Sitting in it and chatting amongst themselves were six men who looked vaguely familiar. It dawned on me that I had seen their photographs in the files Mycroft Holmes had given us with summary information and photos of the members of the group that leased the house, the ones who styled themselves as the Order of the Fittest. As we passed the kitchen, I observed four members of the domestic staff of the house sitting in silence around the table.

Holmes paused in front of each of the doors and looked in at the people in the rooms, to the consternation of the constable.

"Please, sir, the Inspector is waiting for you. He's just up at the top of the stairs.

Indeed he was.

"Holmes!" he shouted, "What do you know about this?"

"About what, Inspector."

"Here. Take a look!"

He gestured to the open door of one of the bedrooms. I followed Holmes in and, at first, saw nothing overly strange. A man appeared to be sleeping in the bed. As I got closer, I froze and gasped.

Lord Peter Dalgington was lying on his in the bed, dressed in his nightclothes. He appeared to be asleep, but under this neck, there was a large dark pool of blood. His head, while still in the place it belonged, had been severed from his body.

"Merciful heavens," I exclaimed, "this is horrible."

Holmes had bent over the corpse and was examining him. He turned to Lestrade.

"Is he the only one?"

"No. There are three more. Every one of them had his head cut off in the middle of the night."

"And might the other four," said Holmes, "be Fernsby, Fitz Leigh, and Olleitch."

"Yes, and since you spent the better part of a year trying to send them off to prison and failed, I think you know more about them than anyone else. Right? And so, you better get to work and figure out who did this."

"Perhaps," said Holmes, "You can assist me by telling me what you know so far as to what took place."

"What we know," said Lestrade, "is the dead men stayed here in this club last night. The staff brought their breakfasts up to them, but they did not answer the knock on their doors, so the trays were left in the hall by their doors. The fifth fellow, Mr. Oliver Glasshover, does take his breakfast, and when he gets up to use the lavatory, he sees that his colleagues' trays are sitting on the floor untouched. He knocks on this door first, gets no answer, and so he opens it and finds His Lordship dead in his bed. He starts screaming bloody murder, and straight away, some of the other members of the house and the staff come running up and check the other rooms and find three more. All dispatched the same way. They go running out of the house, hollering for the police. The nearest officer comes, and he sends straightaway for me, and I get here and send for you. That's the long and short of it, Holmes."

"When did it happen? Did anyone hear anything?"

"Not a thing. All done without making a sound and without turning up the lamps. We think there was two of them. One puts a pillow over the head and forces it back, exposing the neck. And the very next instant, the second one slices his head off. The doctor can give you a better idea of how long they've been dead, but for my experience, I would say they were done in not long after midnight."

I mumbled my agreement.

"Were the doors still locked?" asked Holmes.

"The back door was open. They must have had a key, or they were a clever as you are, Holmes, at picking a lock, and I doubt that."

"A reasonable deduction, Inspector. And none of the other members of the house—those who were not connected to the charity—were harmed in any way? Is that correct?"

"Right. They're the toffs sitting in the library. We told them they had to stay there until we were done with them. None of them objected, which means, I gather, that none of them have jobs they have to go to on Monday morning. You can interrogate them if you want to."

"I do not believe that will be necessary," said Holmes. "I shall concentrate on inspecting the rooms and the premises."

During the next hour, Holmes inspected the bedrooms and the rest of the house. Except for the bodies in the beds, the rooms were undisturbed. Nothing of value had been taken or even touched. When he had finished, he returned to see Inspector Lestrade.

"Well, Holmes, what did you find? Anything we did not notice?"

"The smell in the rooms. Did you notice that?"

"Right. Could not miss it. Even with the odor of a dead body that has evacuated itself, we could smell the faint aroma of curry."

"Precisely. As you know, all of these men had their fingers in the transfers of substantial amounts of money to and back from Calcutta. It is a reasonable hypothesis that being the swindlers they were, they defrauded some party in India, and that party has exacted revenge. In the British Library, you will find books that recount the way the Gurkha tribes dispatched such cheats and thieves by silent decapitation in the middle of the night using a special curved sword. A *Khuku ri* is the name of the sword."

"Right. So, I need to send my men to hunt around London for some Gurkha who smells of curry and might have a nasty sword dangling by his side."

"Yes, but add to that, a connection to the orphans' homes in Calcutta. That should narrow the field somewhat. If the killer possessed a key, it must have been someone who frequented this establishment regularly. That should eliminate all but a few suspects."

"Right, so when can you start?"

"I cannot."

"You what? Why not?"

"Because, my dear Inspector, my services are already engaged by other clients. It will be at least a fortnight before I have time in my schedule to assist you."

"Bloody hell, Holmes. You can tell them that Scotland Yard demands your services, and they can jolly well wait."

"Inasmuch as I wish I could comply, I cannot. If I were to say that my clients have addresses on Downing Street and in Washington DC and they somewhat outrank you, I hope you will understand."

Lestrade glared at Holmes for a moment and then shrugged. "Right. Well, if that is the way it is, then that is the way it will have to be. Thank you for your insight into the evidence."

He turned away from us and went to chat with his officers.

Holmes quickly descended the stairs and started toward the door, but he stopped and entered the parlor. He walked directly to where Oliver Glasshover was sitting. The miserable fellow looked up at Holmes and met his gaze. He nodded at Holmes, and he nodded back.

Holmes then departed the house, and I followed him out to the pavement where we hailed a cab back to Baker Street. Once inside, I was bursting with questions, but he held his one hand up and pressed the index finger of his other hand against his lips, letting me know that I was to remain silent.

I did so, at least until we were back in the familiar room when I could no longer contain myself.

"Holmes! For heaven's sake, you have been consumed with this case for a year. I cannot believe that you are now just going to drop it and hand it over to Lestrade."

"I have no choice."

"Of course, you do. The requests you had from Washington and Number Eleven were trivial. You could have them done in a day. And there cannot be more than one or two curry-smelling Gurkha assassins who have been doing business with those charity chaps. You could track them down on the second day."

"But if they did not have a key, that would take more time to identify them."

"But you said they must have had a key."

"No, my dear Watson, I did not. Lestrade said that. There is, if you will recall, a small window in the basement level that allows one to enter unobserved."

"Well, yes, Holmes. But only someone who is much skinnier than you or me."

"Precisely. And, once inside, that person could then open the back door and let in the accomplice."

"Fine, so one skinny Indian and one who can swing a sword. Both smelling of curry."

"Whoever killed them did not smell of curry."

"What? But we both smelled it. So did Lestrade."

"Small batches of curry powder had been sprinkled in hidden places. It was a ruse."

"Oh, I did not notice that."

"Neither did Lestrade."

"But the sword. It was a ritual beheading by someone who knew how."

"Was it? The *Khutu ri* sword is curved so that it slices as it is drawn across an enemy's throat. Were those necks sliced?"

I was stymied, and I had to think back to the appearance of the cuts on the necks.

164

"No. No. They were not. The wound looked more like it had been chopped, like it would have it been hit by an ax."

"Correct," he said and slowly lit a cigarette. "And for that reason, I no longer feel compelled to investigate the case."

"Holmes! Have you gone mad? That makes no sense at all. Do you have some reason for now wanting to protect a crazed lumberjack who is swinging his ax at people's heads in the middle of the night?"

"I suspect, my dear friend, that it was not an ax but a weapon that performed something like an ax."

"What?"

He took a long pull on his cigarette and slowly exhaled.

"Most likely, a meat cleaver."

I was utterly bewildered … and then I wasn't. My mouth dropped open.

"You cannot mean that it was—"

"Yes, it was."

"With the help of—"

"Precisely."

Dear Sherlockian Readers:

Two historical events provided the setting for this story. The first was suggested to me by an excellent recent book, *The People, No: A Brief History of Anti-Populism* by Thomas Frank. He is one of my favorite political analysts and in the book, he recounted the events leading up to the American election of 1896, including the rise of William Jennings Bryan, the candidate for both the Democratic and Populist Parties. Bryan campaigned on the call for moving the US away from the 'gold only' standard to the 'bi-metallic' that would add silver as a backstop for the US dollar. You can read about it in Frank's book. The parallels to today are fascinating.

Bryan was viciously attacked by the monied classes of New England. Below are just two of the cartoons printed in one of the popular magazines of the time, comparing Bryan to Satan and a murdering rapist of Lady Liberty.

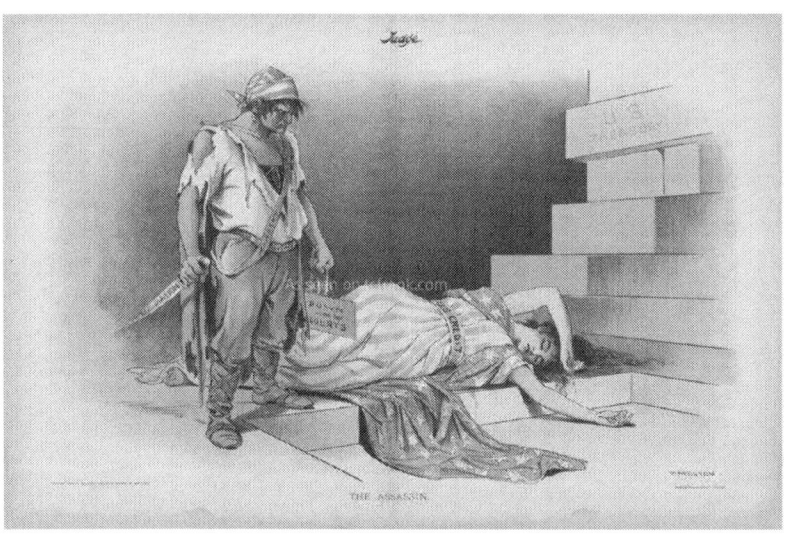

The second event was the attempt by the Hunt brothers in 1980 to corner the global silver market. They almost succeeded and would have made a fortune had not the Commodity Exchange changed the rules.

I borrowed from both of these unusual events to give the villains a unique crime in the Victorian era.

During the years that I served as an executive of a humanitarian aid organization, I had the opportunity to visit Calcutta (now Kolkata) numerous times. I gained the highest possible respect for the people I met there who were operating programs to assist very poor children.

In the late 1890s and through into the first decade of the twentieth century, groups of intellectuals emerged in England, France, Germany and America who made claims for 'scientific racism' based on the 'Social Darwinism' interpretation of the work of Charles Darwin. They advocated for systematic eugenics and economic and social discrimination between races and classes. Their descendants are still with us.

The two economists named in this story are historical figures. Alfred Marshall and Arthur Pigou both had distinguished careers in British political life.

The Royal Albert Hall was opened in 1871 and dedicated by Queen Victoria to the memory of her husband. For years it was plagued by an acoustic echo, which has since been fixed. Each summer, a series of concerts—The Proms—are held there, culminating in the *Last Night of the Proms* when several patriotic British songs are played, accompanied by the joyful, raucous singing, flag waving, and celebrations of thousands of English men and women. The concert in this story borrows from that event.

The names and places in the story are accurate, to the best of my ability, for London and Sussex in the 1890s.

Warm regards,   Craig

About the Author

In May of 2014 the Sherlock Holmes Society of Canada – better known as The Bootmakers – announced a contest for a new Sherlock Holmes story. Although he had no experience writing fiction, the author submitted a short Sherlock Holmes mystery and was blessed to be declared one of the winners. Thus inspired, he has continued to write new Sherlock Holmes Mysteries since and is on a mission to write a new story as a tribute to each of the sixty stories in the original Canon. He has been writing these stories while living in Toronto, Buenos Aires, Tokyo, Bahrain, the Okanagan, and Manhattan. Several readers of New Sherlock Holmes Mysteries have kindly sent him suggestions for future stories. You are welcome to do likewise at craigstephencopland@gmail.com.

More Historical Mysteries
by Craig Stephen Copland
www.SherlockHolmesMystery.com

Open website to look inside and download

 ***Studying Scarlet.*** Starlet O'Halloran, a fabulous mature woman, who reminds the reader of Scarlet O'Hara (but who, for copyright reasons cannot actually be her) has arrived in London looking for her long-lost husband, Brett (who resembles Rhett Butler, but who, for copyright reasons, cannot actually be him). She enlists the help of Sherlock Holmes. This is an unauthorized parody, inspired by Arthur Conan Doyle's *A Study in Scarlet* and Margaret Mitchell's *Gone with the Wind.*

 ***The Sign of the Third.*** Fifteen hundred years ago, the courageous Princess Hemamali smuggled the sacred tooth of the Buddha into Ceylon. Now, for the first time, it is being brought to London to be part of a magnificent exhibit at the British Museum. But what if something were to happen to it? It would be a disaster for the British Empire. Sherlock Holmes, Dr. Watson, and even Mycroft Holmes are called upon to prevent such a crisis. This novella is inspired by the Sherlock Holmes mystery, The Sign of the Four.

 ***A Sandal from East Anglia.*** Archeological excavations at an old abbey unearth an ancient document that has the potential to change the course of the British Empire and all of Christendom. Holmes encounters some evil young men and a strikingly beautiful young Sister, with a curious double life. The mystery is inspired by the original Sherlock Holmes story, *A Scandal in Bohemia*

The Bald-Headed Trust. Watson insists on taking Sherlock Holmes on a short vacation to the seaside in Plymouth. No sooner has Holmes arrived than he is needed to solve a double murder and prevent a massive fraud diabolically designed by the evil Professor himself. Who knew that a family of devout conservative churchgoers could come to the aid of Sherlock Holmes and bring enormous grief to evildoers? The story is inspired by *The Red-Headed League.*

A Case of Identity Theft. It is the fall of 1888, and Jack the Ripper is terrorizing London. A young married couple is found, minus their heads. Sherlock Holmes, Dr. Watson, the couple's mothers, and Mycroft must join forces to find the murderer before he kills again and makes off with half a million pounds. The novella is a tribute to A Case of Identity. It will appeal both to devoted fans of Sherlock Holmes, as well as to those who love the great game of rugby

The Hudson Valley Mystery. A young man in New York went mad and murdered his father. His mother believes he is innocent and knows he is not crazy. She appeals to Sherlock Holmes and, together with Dr. and Mrs. Watson, he crosses the Atlantic to help this client in need. This new story was inspired by *The Boscombe Valley*

The Mystery of the Five Oranges. A desperate father enters 221B Baker Street. His daughter has been kidnapped and spirited off to North America. The evil network who have taken her has spies everywhere. There is only one hope – Sherlock Holmes. Sherlockians will enjoy this new adventure, inspired by The Five Orange Pips and Anne of Green Gables.

www.SherlockHolmesMystery.com

The Man Who Was Twisted But Hip. France is torn apart by The Dreyfus Affair. Westminster needs Sherlock Holmes so that the evil tide of anti-Semitism that has engulfed France will not spread. Sherlock and Watson go to Paris to solve the mystery and thwart Moriarty. This new mystery is inspired by *The Man with the Twisted Lip,* as well as by *The Hunchback of Notre Dame*

The Adventure of the Blue Belt Buckle. A young street urchin discovers a man's belt and buckle under a bush in Hyde Park. A body is found in a hotel room in Mayfair. Scotland Yard seeks the help of Sherlock Holmes in solving the murder. The Queen's Jubilee could be ruined. Sherlock Holmes, Dr. Watson, Scotland Yard, and Her Majesty all team up to prevent a crime of unspeakable dimensions. A new mystery inspired by *The Blue Carbuncle.*

The Adventure of the Spectred Bat. A beautiful young woman, just weeks away from giving birth, arrives at Baker Street in the middle of the night. Her sister was attacked by a bat and died, and now it is attacking her. A vampire? The story is a tribute to *The Adventure of the Speckled Band* and, like the original, leaves the mind wondering and the heart racing.

The Adventure of the Engineer's Mom. A brilliant young Cambridge University engineer is carrying out secret research for the Admiralty. It will lead to the building of the world's most powerful battleship, The Dreadnaught. His adventuress mother is kidnapped, and he seeks the help of Sherlock Holmes. This new mystery is a tribute to *The Engineer's Thumb.*

<u>www.SherlockHolmesMystery.com</u>

The Adventure of the Notable Bachelorette. A snobbish nobleman enters 221B Baker Street, demanding the help in finding his much younger wife – a beautiful and spirited American from the West. Three days later, the wife is accused of a vile crime. Now she comes to Sherlock Holmes seeking to prove her innocence. This new mystery was inspired by *The Adventure of the Noble Bachelor.*

The Adventure of the Beryl Anarchists. A deeply distressed banker enters 221B Baker St. His safe has been robbed, and he is certain that his motorcycle-riding sons have betrayed him. Highly incriminating and embarrassing records of the financial and personal affairs of England's nobility are now in the hands of blackmailers. Then a young girl is murdered. A tribute to *The Adventure of the Beryl Coronet.*

The Adventure of the Coiffured Bitches. A beautiful young woman will soon inherit a lot of money. She disappears. Another young woman finds out far too much and, in desperation, seeks help. Sherlock Holmes, Dr. Watson, and Miss Violet Hunter must solve the mystery of the coiffured bitches and avoid the massive mastiff that could tear their throats out. A tribute to *The Adventure of the Copper Beeches*

The Silver Horse, Braised. The greatest horse race of the century will take place at Epsom Downs. Millions have been bet. Owners, jockeys, grooms, and gamblers from across England and America arrive. Jockeys and horses are killed. Holmes fails to solve the crime until… This mystery is a tribute to *Silver Blaze* and the great racetrack stories of Damon Runyon.

 **The Box of Cards.** A brother and a sister from a strict religious family disappear. The parents are alarmed, but Scotland Yard says they are just off sowing their wild oats. A horrific, gruesome package arrives in the post, and it becomes clear that a terrible crime is in process. Sherlock Holmes is called in to help. A tribute to *The Cardboard Box*

 **The Yellow Farce.** Sherlock Holmes is sent to Japan. The war between Russia and Japan is raging. Alliances between countries in these years before World War I are fragile, and any misstep could plunge the world into Armageddon. The wife of the British ambassador is suspected of being a Russian agent. Join Holmes and Watson as they travel around the world to Japan. Inspired by *The Yellow Face*.

 **The Stock Market Murders.** A young man's friend has gone missing. Two more bodies of young men turn up. All are tied to The City and to one of the greatest frauds ever visited upon the citizens of England. The story is based on the true story of James Whitaker Wright and is inspired by *The Stock Broker's Clerk*. Any resemblance of the villain to a certain American political figure is entirely coincidental.

 **The Glorious Yacht.** On the night of April 12, 1912, off the coast of Newfoundland, one of the greatest disasters of all time took place – the Unsinkable Titanic struck an iceberg and sank with a horrendous loss of life. The news of the disaster leads Holmes and Watson to reminisce about one of their earliest adventures. It began as a sailing race and ended as a tale of murder, kidnapping, piracy, and survival through a tempest. A tribute to *The Gloria Scott*.

A Most Grave Ritual. In 1649, King Charles I escaped and made a desperate run for Continent. Did he leave behind a vast fortune? The patriarch of an ancient Royalist family dies in the courtyard, and the locals believe that the headless ghost of the king did him in. The police accuse his son of murder. Sherlock Holmes is hired to exonerate the lad. A tribute to *The Musgrave Ritual*

The Spy Gate Liars. Dr. Watson receives an urgent telegram telling him that Sherlock Holmes is in France and near death. He rushes to aid his dear friend, only to find that what began as a doctor's housecall has turned into yet another adventure as Sherlock Holmes races to keep an unknown ruthless murderer from dispatching yet another former German army officer. A tribute to *The Reigate Squires.*

The Cuckold Man Colonel James Barclay needs the help of Sherlock Holmes. His exceptionally beautiful, but much younger, wife has disappeared, and foul play is suspected. Has she been kidnapped and held for ransom? Or is she in the clutches of a deviant monster? The story is a tribute not only to the original mystery, *The Crooked Man*, but also to the biblical story of King David and Bathsheba

The Impatient Dissidents. In March 1881, the Czar of Russia was assassinated by anarchists. That summer, an attempt was made to murder his daughter, Maria, the wife of England's Prince Alfred. A Russian Count is found dead in a hospital in London. Scotland Yard and the Home Office arrive at 221B and enlist the help of Sherlock Holmes to track down the killers and stop them. This new mystery is a tribute to *The Resident Patient.*

The Grecian, Earned. This story picks up where *The Greek Interpreter* left off. The villains of that story were murdered in Budapest, and so Holmes and Watson set off in search of "the Grecian girl" to solve the mystery. What they discover is a massive plot involving the re-birth of the Olympic games in 1896 and a colorful cast of characters at home and on the Continent.

The Three Rhodes Not Taken. Oxford University is famous for its passionate pursuit of learning. The Rhodes Scholarship has been recently established, and some men are prepared to lie, steal, slander, and, maybe murder, in the pursuit of it. Sherlock Holmes is called upon to track down a thief who has stolen vital documents pertaining to the winner of the scholarship, but what will he do when the prime suspect is found dead? A tribute to *The Three Students*

The Naval Knaves. On September 15, 1894, an anarchist attempted to bomb the Greenwich Observatory. He failed, but the attempt led Sherlock Holmes into an intricate web of spies, foreign naval officers, and a beautiful princess. Once again, suspicion landed on poor Percy Phelps, now working in a senior position in the Admiralty, and once again, Holmes has to use both his powers of deduction and raw courage to not only rescue Percy but to prevent an unspeakable disaster. A tribute to *The Naval Treaty.*

A Scandal in Trumplandia. NOT a new mystery but a political satire. The story is a parody of the much-loved original story, *A Scandal in Bohemia*, with the character of the King of Bohemia replaced by you-know-who. If you enjoy both political satire and Sherlock Holmes, you will get a chuckle out of this new story.

The Binomial Asteroid Problem. The deadly final encounter between Professor Moriarty and Sherlock Holmes took place at Reichenbach Falls. But when was their first encounter? This new story answers that question. What began a stolen Gladstone bag escalates into murder and more. This new story is a tribute to *The Adventure of the Final Problem.*

The Adventure of Charlotte Europa Golderton. *Charles Augustus Milverton* was shot and sent to his just reward. But now another diabolical scheme of blackmail has emerged centered in the telegraph offices of the Royal Mail. It is linked to an archeological expedition whose director disappeared. Someone is prepared to murder to protect their ill-gotten gain and possibly steal a priceless treasure. Holmes is hired by not one but three women who need his help.

The Mystery of 222 Baker Street. The body of a Scotland Yard inspector is found in a locked room in 222 Baker Street. There is no clue as to how he died. Then another murder in the very same room. Holmes and Watson might have to offer themselves as potential victims if the culprits are to be discovered. A tribute to the original Sherlock Holmes story, *The Adventure of the Empty House*

The Adventure of the Norwood Rembrandt. A man facing execution appeals to Sherlock Holmes to save him. He claims that he is innocent. Holmes agrees to take on his case. Five years ago, he was convicted of the largest theft of art masterpieces in British history, and of murdering the butler who tried to stop him. Holmes and Watson have to find the real murderer and the missing works of art --- if the client is innocent after all. A tribute to *The Adventure of the Norwood Builder* in the original Canon.

The Horror of the Bastard's Villa. A Scottish clergyman and his faithful border collie visit 221B and tell a tale of a ghostly Banshee on the Isle of Skye. After the specter appeared, two people died. Holmes sends Watson on ahead to investigate and report. More terrifying horrors occur, and Sherlock Holmes must come and solve the awful mystery before more people are murdered. A tribute to the original story in the Canon, Arthur Conan Doyle's masterpiece, *The Hound of the Baskervilles* .

The Dancer from the Dance. In 1909 the entire world of dance changed when Les Ballets Russes opened in Paris. They also made annual visits to the West End in London. Tragically, during their 1913 tour, two of their dancers are found murdered. Sherlock Holmes is brought into to find the murderer and prevent any more killings. The story adheres fairly closely to the history of ballet and is a tribute to the original story in the Canon, *The Adventure of the Dancing Men.*

The Solitary Bicycle Thief. Remember Violet Smith, the beautiful young woman whom Sherlock Holmes and Dr. Watson rescued from a forced marriage, as recorded in *The Adventure of the Solitary Cyclist*? Ten years later, she and Cyril reappear in 221B Baker Street with a strange tale of the theft of their bicycles. What on the surface seemed like a trifle turns out to be the door that leads Sherlock Holmes into a web of human trafficking, espionage, blackmail, and murder. A new and powerful cabal of master criminals has formed in London, and they will stop at nothing, not even the murder of an innocent foreign student, to extend the hold on the criminal underworld of London

www.SherlockHolmesMystery.com

The Adventure of the Prioress's Tale. The senior field hockey team from an elite girls' school goes to Dover for a beach holiday … and disappears. Have they been abducted into white slavery? Did they run off to Paris? Are they being held for ransom? Can Sherlock Holmes find them in time? Holmes, Watson, Lestrade, the Prioress of the school, and a new gang of Irregulars must find them before something terrible happens. a tribute to *The Adventure of the Priory School in the Canon.*

The Adventure of Mrs. J.L. Heber. A mad woman is murdering London bachelors by driving a railway spike through their heads. Scotland Yard demands that Sherlock Holmes help them find and stop a crazed murderess who is re-enacting the biblical murders by Jael. Holmes agrees and finds that revenge is being taken for deeds treachery and betrayal that took place ten years ago in the Rocky Mountains of Canada. Holmes, Watson, and Lestrade must move quickly before more men and women lose their lives. The story is a tribute to the original Sherlock Holmes story, *The Adventure of Black Peter.*

The Return of Napoleon. In October 1805, Napoleon's fleet was defeated in the Battle of Trafalgar. Now his ghost has returned to England for the centenary of the battle, intent on wreaking revenge on the descendants of Admiral Horatio Nelson and on all of England. The mother of the great-great-grandchildren of Admiral Nelson contacts Sherlock Holmes, needing his help. First, Dr. Watson comes to the manor, and he meets not only the lovely children but also finds that something apparently supernatural is going on. Holmes assumes that some mad Frenchmen, intent on avenging Napoleon, are conspiring to wreak havoc on England and possibly threatening the children. Watson believes that something terrifying and occult may be at work. Neither is prepared for the true target of the Napoleonists, or of the Emperor's ghost

 ***The Adventure of the Pinched Palimpsest.*** A professor has been proselytizing for anarchism. Three students fall for his doctrines and engage in direct action by stealing priceless artifacts from the British Museum, returning them to the oppressed people from whom their colonial masters stole them. In the midst of their caper, a museum guard is shot dead, and they are charged with the murder. After being persuaded by a vulnerable friend of the students, Sherlock Holmes agrees to take on the case. He soon discovers that no one involved is telling the complete truth. Join Holmes and Watson as they race from London to Oxford, then to Cambridge and finally up to a remote village in Scotland and seek to discover the clues that are tied to an obscure medieval palimpsest.

 ***The Adventure of the Missing Better Half.*** Did you ever wonder what happened to Godfrey Staunton, the missing Three-Quarter, after Holmes found him? This story tells you. He met an exceptional young woman, fell in love, and got married. He was chosen to play on England's National Team in the 1899 Home Nations Championship games. Life was good. ... and then it got much worse. Together -- Godfrey Staunton, Dr. Leslie Armstrong, Dr. Watson, and Sherlock Holmes -- must stop an unspeakable crime taking place. This 38th New Sherlock Holmes. A tribute to *The Adventure of the Missing Three Quarter.*

 ***The Inequality of Mercy.*** What happened after Sherlock Holmes and Dr. Watson pardoned Captain Jack Croker for killing Sir Eustace at the Abbey Grange. Have you imagined that he sailed the seven seas for a year and then returned to his beautiful, beloved Mary Fraser? That didn't happen. A year later, murder, treachery, and international intrigue descended on Abbey Grange, and, once again, Sherlock Holmes was called upon to bring criminals to justice and assist in the course of true love. Buy the story now, and find out what happened.

The Adventure of the Second Entente. In June of 1901, a wealthy young nobleman is murdered, and yet again, Scotland Yard requires help from Sherlock Holmes. The baron has recently returned from an expedition searching for oil in Persia. His only relative and sole heir, a woman from California is the obvious suspect. But then she comes to Sherlock Holmes desperately seeking his help. If she did not kill the man, then who did? Join Holmes, Watson and an unusual woman as they seek to solve the crime and avoid becoming victims themselves. The story is a tribute to the original Sherlock Holmes mystery, *The Adventure of the Second Stain.*

The Adventure of the Morning Glory Murders. Sherlock Holmes confronts the horrible racial and religious prejudice that was rampant in the Victorian era and helps the heroic victims of those evils discover a new life.A family from Argentina has disappeared and it is feared that they were abducted. Their lives are in danger. The father, a colonel in the Argentine army has enemies from years ago that may be seeking revenge. The gigantic 'mulatto' who was the cook in the story about Wisteria Lodge (remember him?) is falsely accused. With his help, Sherlock Holmes must find the family before it is too late.If reading about the prejudices of the Victorian era -- many of which appeared in the original Sherlock Holmes stories -- upsets you, this is not for you. However, if you want to read about how brave people faced those evils and overcame them, this is a story you will enjoy.

www.SherlockHolmesMystery.com

Contributions to
The Great Game of
Sherlockian Scholarship

Sherlock and Barack. This is NOT a new Sherlock Holmes Mystery. It is a Sherlockian research monograph. Why did Barack Obama win in November 2012? Why did Mitt Romney lose? Pundits and political scientists have offered countless reasons. This book reveals the truth - The Sherlock Holmes Factor. Had it not been for Sherlock Holmes, Mitt Romney would be president.

From The Beryl Coronet to Vimy Ridge. This is NOT a New Sherlock Holmes Mystery. It is a monograph of Sherlockian research. This new monograph in the Great Game of Sherlockian scholarship argues that there was a Sherlock Holmes factor in the causes of World War I... and that it is secretly revealed in the *roman a clef* story that we know as *The Adventure of the Beryl Coronet*

www.SherlockHolmesMystery.com

Reverend Ezekiel Black—'The Sherlock Holmes of the American West'—Mystery Stories.

A Scarlet Trail of Murder. At ten o'clock on Sunday morning, the twenty-second of October, 1882, in an abandoned house in the West Bottom of Kansas City, a fellow named Jasper Harrison did not wake up. His inability to do was the result of his having had his throat cut. The Reverend Mr. Ezekiel Black, a part-time Methodist minister, and an itinerant US Marshall is called in. This original western mystery was inspired by the great Sherlock Holmes classic, *A Study in Scarlet*

The Brand of the Flying Four. This case all began one quiet evening in a room in Kansas City. A few weeks later, a gruesome murder, took place in Denver. By the time Rev. Black had solved the mystery, justice, of the frontier variety, not the courtroom, had been meted out. The story is inspired by *The Sign of the Four* by Arthur Conan Doyle, and like that story, it combines murder most foul, and romance most enticing.

www.SherlockHolmesMystery.com

Collection Sets for eBooks and paperback are available at *40% off the price of buying them separately.*

Collection One
The Sign of the Tooth
The Hudson Valley Mystery
A Case of Identity Theft
The Bald-Headed Trust
Studying Scarlet
The Mystery of the Five Oranges

Collection Two
A Sandal from East Anglia
The Man Who Was Twisted But Hip
The Blue Belt Buckle
The Spectred Bat

Collection Three
The Engineer's Mom
The Notable Bachelorette
The Beryl Anarchists
The Coiffured Bitches

Collection Four

The Silver Horse, Braised
The Box of Cards
The Yellow Farce
The Three Rhodes Not Taken

Collection Five

The Stock Market Murders
The Glorious Yacht
The Most Grave Ritual
The Spy Gate Liars

Collection Six

The Cuckold Man
The Impatient Dissidents
The Grecian, Earned
The Naval Knaves

Collection Seven

The Binomial Asteroid Problem
The Mystery of 222 Baker Street
The Adventure of Charlotte Europa Golderton
The Adventure of the Norwood Rembrandt

Collection Eight

The Dancer from the Dance
The Adventure of the Prioress's Tale
The Adventure of Mrs. J. L. Heber
The Solitary Bicycle Thief

Collection Nine

The Adventure of Charlotte Europa Golderton

The Return of Napoleon

The Adventure of the Pinched Palimpsest

The Adventure of the Missing Better Half

Super Collections A and B

40 New Sherlock Holmes Mysteries.

The perfect ebooks for readers who can only borrow one book a month from Amazon

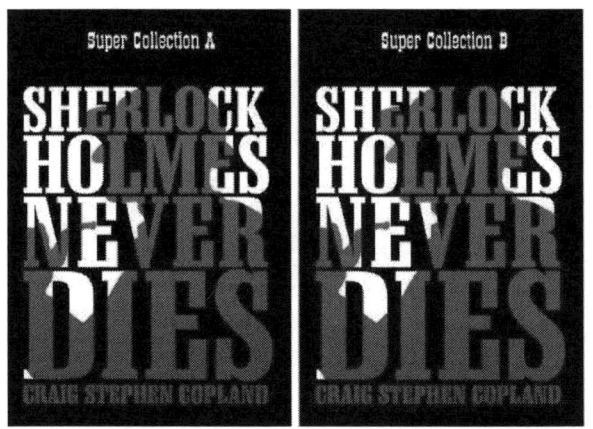

www.SherlockHolmesMystery.com

The Adventure
of the Bruce-Partington
Plans

The Original Sherlock Holmes Story

Arthur Conan Doyle

The Adventure of the Bruce-Partington Plans

In the third week of November, in the year 1895, a dense yellow fog settled down upon London. From the Monday to the Thursday I doubt whether it was ever possible from our windows in Baker Street to see the loom of the opposite houses. The first day Holmes had spent in cross-indexing his huge book of references. The second and third had been patiently occupied upon a subject which he had recently made his hobby--the music of the Middle Ages. But when, for the fourth time, after pushing back our chairs from breakfast we saw the greasy, heavy brown swirl still drifting past us and condensing in oily drops upon the window-panes, my comrade's impatient and active nature could endure this drab existence no longer. He paced restlessly about our sitting-room in a fever of suppressed energy, biting his nails, tapping the furniture, and chafing against inaction.

"Nothing of interest in the paper, Watson?" he said.

I was aware that by anything of interest, Holmes meant anything of criminal interest. There was the news of a revolution, of a possible war, and of an impending change of government; but these did not come within the horizon of my companion. I could see nothing recorded in the shape of crime which was not commonplace and futile. Holmes groaned and resumed his restless meanderings.

"The London criminal is certainly a dull fellow," said he in the querulous voice of the sportsman whose game has failed him. "Look out this window, Watson. See how the figures loom up, are dimly seen, and then blend once more into the cloud-bank. The thief or the murderer could roam London on such a day as the tiger does the jungle, unseen until he pounces, and then evident only to his victim."

"There have," said I, "been numerous petty thefts."

Holmes snorted his contempt.

"This great and sombre stage is set for something more worthy than that," said he. "It is fortunate for this community that I am not a criminal."

"It is, indeed!" said I heartily.

"Suppose that I were Brooks or Woodhouse, or any of the fifty men who have good reason for taking my life, how long could I survive against my own pursuit? A summons, a bogus appointment, and all would be over. It is well they don't have days of fog in the Latin countries--the countries of assassination. By Jove! here comes something at last to break our dead monotony."

It was the maid with a telegram. Holmes tore it open and burst out laughing.

"Well, well! What next?" said he. "Brother Mycroft is coming round."

"Why not?" I asked.

"Why not? It is as if you met a tram-car coming down a country lane. Mycroft has his rails and he runs on them. His Pall Mall lodgings, the Diogenes Club, Whitehall--that is his cycle. Once, and only once, he has been here. What upheaval can possibly have derailed him?"

"Does he not explain?"

Holmes handed me his brother's telegram.

```
"Must see you over Cadogan West. Coming at
once."
```

"Cadogan West? I have heard the name."

"It recalls nothing to my mind. But that Mycroft should break out in this erratic fashion! A planet might as well leave its orbit. By the way, do you know what Mycroft is?"

I had some vague recollection of an explanation at the time of the Adventure of the Greek Interpreter.

"You told me that he had some small office under the British government."

Holmes chuckled.

"I did not know you quite so well in those days. One has to be discreet when one talks of high matters of state. You are right in thinking that he is under the British government. You would also be right in a sense if you said that occasionally he IS the British government."

"My dear Holmes!"

"I thought I might surprise you. Mycroft draws four hundred and fifty pounds a year, remains a subordinate, has no ambitions of any kind, will receive neither honour nor title, but remains the most indispensable man in the country."

"But how?"

"Well, his position is unique. He has made it for himself. There has never been anything like it before, nor will be again. He has the tidiest and most orderly brain, with the greatest capacity for storing facts, of any man living. The same great powers which I have turned to the detection of crime he has used for this particular business. The conclusions of every department are passed to him, and he is the central exchange, the clearinghouse, which makes out the balance. All other men are specialists, but his specialism is omniscience. We will suppose that a minister needs information as to a point which involves the Navy, India, Canada and the bimetallic question; he could get his separate advices from various departments upon each, but only Mycroft can focus them all, and say offhand how each factor would affect the other. They began by using him as a short-cut, a convenience; now he has made himself an essential. In that great brain of his everything is pigeon-holed and can be handed out in an instant. Again and again his word has decided the national policy. He lives in it. He thinks of nothing else save when, as an intellectual exercise, he unbends if I call upon him and ask him to advise me on one of my little problems. But Jupiter is descending to-day. What on earth can it mean? Who is Cadogan West, and what is he to Mycroft?"

"I have it," I cried, and plunged among the litter of papers upon the sofa. "Yes, yes, here he is, sure enough! Cadogan West was the young man who was found dead on the Underground on Tuesday morning."

Holmes sat up at attention, his pipe halfway to his lips.

"This must be serious, Watson. A death which has caused my brother to alter his habits can be no ordinary one. What in the world can he have to do with it? The case was featureless as I remember it. The young man had apparently fallen out of the train and killed himself. He had not been robbed, and there was no particular reason to suspect violence. Is that not so?"

"There has been an inquest," said I, "and a good many fresh facts have come out. Looked at more closely, I should certainly say that it was a curious case."

"Judging by its effect upon my brother, I should think it must be a most extraordinary one." He snuggled down in his armchair. "Now, Watson, let us have the facts."

"The man's name was Arthur Cadogan West. He was twenty-seven years of age, unmarried, and a clerk at Woolwich Arsenal."

"Government employ. Behold the link with Brother Mycroft!"

"He left Woolwich suddenly on Monday night. Was last seen by his fiancee, Miss Violet Westbury, whom he left abruptly in the fog about 7:30 that evening. There was no quarrel between them and she can give no motive for his action. The next thing heard of him was when his dead body was discovered by a plate-layer named Mason, just outside Aldgate Station on the Underground system in London."

"When?"

"The body was found at six on Tuesday morning. It was lying wide of the metals upon the left hand of the track as one goes eastward, at a point close to the station, where the line emerges from the tunnel in which it runs. The head was badly crushed--an injury which might well have been caused by a fall from the train. The body could only have come on the line in that way. Had it been carried down from any neighbouring street, it must have passed the station barriers, where a collector is always standing. This point seems absolutely certain."

"Very good. The case is definite enough. The man, dead or alive, either fell or was precipitated from a train. So much is clear to me. Continue."

"The trains which traverse the lines of rail beside which the body was found are those which run from west to east, some being purely Metropolitan, and some from Willesden and outlying junctions. It can be stated for certain that this young man, when he met his death, was travelling in this direction at some late hour of the night, but at what point he entered the train it is impossible to state."

"His ticket, of course, would show that."

"There was no ticket in his pockets."

"No ticket! Dear me, Watson, this is really very singular. According to my experience it is not possible to reach the platform of a Metropolitan train without exhibiting one's ticket. Presumably, then, the young man had one. Was it taken from him in order to conceal the station from which he came? It is possible. Or did he drop it in the carriage? That is also possible. But the point is of curious interest. I understand that there was no sign of robbery?"

"Apparently not. There is a list here of his possessions. His purse contained two pounds fifteen. He had also a check-book on the Woolwich branch of the Capital and Counties Bank. Through this his identity was established. There were also two dress-circle tickets for the Woolwich Theatre, dated for that very evening. Also a small packet of technical papers."

Holmes gave an exclamation of satisfaction.

"There we have it at last, Watson! British government--Woolwich. Arsenal--technical papers--Brother Mycroft, the chain is complete. But here he comes, if I am not mistaken, to speak for himself."

A moment later the tall and portly form of Mycroft Holmes was ushered into the room. Heavily built and massive, there was a suggestion of uncouth physical inertia in the figure, but above this unwieldy frame there was perched a head so masterful in its brow, so alert in its steel-gray, deep-set eyes, so firm in its lips, and so subtle in its play of expression, that after the first glance one forgot the gross body and remembered only the dominant mind.

At his heels came our old friend Lestrade, of Scotland Yard--thin and austere. The gravity of both their faces foretold some weighty quest. The detective shook hands without a word. Mycroft Holmes struggled out of his overcoat and subsided into an armchair.

"A most annoying business, Sherlock," said he. "I extremely dislike altering my habits, but the powers that be would take no denial. In the present state of Siam it is most awkward that I should be away from the office. But it is a real crisis. I have never seen the Prime Minister so upset. As to the Admiralty--it is buzzing like an overturned bee-hive. Have you read up the case?"

"We have just done so. What were the technical papers?"

"Ah, there's the point! Fortunately, it has not come out. The press would be furious if it did. The papers which this wretched youth had in his pocket were the plans of the Bruce-Partington submarine."

Mycroft Holmes spoke with a solemnity which showed his sense of the importance of the subject. His brother and I sat expectant.

"Surely you have heard of it? I thought everyone had heard of it."

"Only as a name."

"Its importance can hardly be exaggerated. It has been the most jealously guarded of all government secrets. You may take it from me that naval warfare becomes impossible within the radius of a Bruce-Partington's operation. Two years ago a very large sum was smuggled through the Estimates and was expended in acquiring a monopoly of the invention. Every effort has been made to keep the secret. The plans, which are exceedingly intricate, comprising some thirty separate patents, each essential to the working of the whole, are kept in an elaborate safe in a confidential office adjoining the arsenal, with burglar-proof doors and windows. Under no conceivable circumstances were the plans to be taken from the office. If the chief constructor of the Navy desired to consult them, even he was forced to go to the Woolwich office for the purpose. And yet here we find them in the pocket of a dead junior clerk in the heart of London. From an official point of view it's simply awful."

"But you have recovered them?"

"No, Sherlock, no! That's the pinch. We have not. Ten papers were taken from Woolwich. There were seven in the pocket of Cadogan West. The three most essential are gone--stolen, vanished. You must drop everything, Sherlock. Never mind your usual petty puzzles of the police-court. It's a vital international problem that you have to solve. Why did Cadogan West take the papers, where are the missing ones, how did he die, how came his body where it was found, how can the evil be set right? Find an answer to all these questions, and you will have done good service for your country."

"Why do you not solve it yourself, Mycroft? You can see as far as I."

"Possibly, Sherlock. But it is a question of getting details. Give me your details, and from an armchair I will return you an excellent expert opinion. But to run here and run there, to cross-question railway guards, and lie on my face with a lens to my eye--it is not my metier. No, you are the one man who can clear the matter up. If you have a fancy to see your name in the next honours list--"

My friend smiled and shook his head.

"I play the game for the game's own sake," said he. "But the problem certainly presents some points of interest, and I shall be very pleased to look into it. Some more facts, please."

"I have jotted down the more essential ones upon this sheet of paper, together with a few addresses which you will find of service. The actual official guardian of the papers is the famous government expert, Sir James Walter, whose decorations and sub-titles fill two lines of a book of reference. He has grown gray in the service, is a gentleman, a favoured guest in the most exalted houses, and, above all, a man whose patriotism is beyond suspicion. He is one of two who have a key of the safe. I may add that the papers were undoubtedly in the office during working hours on Monday, and that Sir James left for London about three o'clock taking his key with him. He was at the house of Admiral Sinclair at Barclay Square during the whole of the evening when this incident occurred."

"Has the fact been verified?"

"Yes; his brother, Colonel Valentine Walter, has testified to his departure from Woolwich, and Admiral Sinclair to his arrival in London; so Sir James is no longer a direct factor in the problem."

"Who was the other man with a key?"

"The senior clerk and draughtsman, Mr. Sidney Johnson. He is a man of forty, married, with five children. He is a silent, morose man, but he has, on the whole, an excellent record in the public service. He is unpopular with his colleagues, but a hard worker. According to his own account, corroborated only by the word of his wife, he was at home the whole of Monday evening after office hours, and his key has never left the watch-chain upon which it hangs."

"Tell us about Cadogan West."

"He has been ten years in the service and has done good work. He has the reputation of being hot-headed and imperious, but a straight, honest man. We have nothing against him. He was next Sidney Johnson in the office. His duties brought him into daily, personal contact with the plans. No one else had the handling of them."

"Who locked up the plans that night?"

"Mr. Sidney Johnson, the senior clerk."

"Well, it is surely perfectly clear who took them away. They are actually found upon the person of this junior clerk, Cadogan West. That seems final, does it not?"

"It does, Sherlock, and yet it leaves so much unexplained. In the first place, why did he take them?"

"I presume they were of value?"

"He could have got several thousands for them very easily."

"Can you suggest any possible motive for taking the papers to London except to sell them?"

"No, I cannot."

"Then we must take that as our working hypothesis. Young West took the papers. Now this could only be done by having a false key--"

"Several false keys. He had to open the building and the room."

"He had, then, several false keys. He took the papers to London to sell the secret, intending, no doubt, to have the plans themselves back in the safe next morning before they were missed. While in London on this treasonable mission he met his end."

"How?"

"We will suppose that he was travelling back to Woolwich when he was killed and thrown out of the compartment."

"Aldgate, where the body was found, is considerably past the station London Bridge, which would be his route to Woolwich."

"Many circumstances could be imagined under which he would pass London Bridge. There was someone in the carriage, for example, with whom he was having an absorbing interview. This interview led to a violent scene in which he lost his life. Possibly he tried to leave the carriage, fell out on the line, and so met his end. The other closed the door. There was a thick fog, and nothing could be seen."

"No better explanation can be given with our present knowledge; and yet consider, Sherlock, how much you leave untouched. We will suppose, for argument's sake, that young Cadogan West HAD determined to convey these papers to London. He would naturally have made an appointment with the foreign agent and kept his evening clear. Instead of that he took two tickets for the theatre, escorted his fiancee halfway there, and then suddenly disappeared."

"A blind," said Lestrade, who had sat listening with some impatience to the conversation.

"A very singular one. That is objection No. 1. Objection No. 2: We will suppose that he reaches London and sees the foreign agent. He must bring back the papers before morning or the loss will be discovered. He took away ten. Only seven were in his pocket. What had become of the other three? He certainly would not leave them of his own free will. Then, again, where is the price of his treason? Once would have expected to find a large sum of money in his pocket."

"It seems to me perfectly clear," said Lestrade. "I have no doubt at all as to what occurred. He took the papers to sell them. He saw the agent. They could not agree as to price. He started home again, but the agent went with him. In the train the agent murdered him, took the more essential papers, and threw his body from the carriage. That would account for everything, would it not?"

"Why had he no ticket?"

"The ticket would have shown which station was nearest the agent's house. Therefore he took it from the murdered man's pocket."

"Good, Lestrade, very good," said Holmes. "Your theory holds together. But if this is true, then the case is at an end. On the one hand, the traitor is dead. On the other, the plans of the Bruce-Partington submarine are presumably already on the Continent. What is there for us to do?"

"To act, Sherlock--to act!" cried Mycroft, springing to his feet. "All my instincts are against this explanation. Use your powers! Go to the scene of the crime! See the people concerned! Leave no stone unturned! In all your career you have never had so great a chance of serving your country."

"Well, well!" said Holmes, shrugging his shoulders. "Come, Watson! And you, Lestrade, could you favour us with your company for an hour or two? We will begin our investigation by a visit to Aldgate Station. Good-bye, Mycroft. I shall let you have a report before evening, but I warn you in advance that you have little to expect."

An hour later Holmes, Lestrade and I stood upon the Underground railroad at the point where it emerges from the tunnel immediately before Aldgate Station. A courteous red-faced old gentleman represented the railway company.

"This is where the young man's body lay," said he, indicating a spot about three feet from the metals. "It could not have fallen from above, for these, as you see, are all blank walls. Therefore, it could only have come from a train, and that train, so far as we can trace it, must have passed about midnight on Monday."

"Have the carriages been examined for any sign of violence?"

"There are no such signs, and no ticket has been found."

"No record of a door being found open?"

"None."

"We have had some fresh evidence this morning," said Lestrade. "A passenger who passed Aldgate in an ordinary Metropolitan train about 11:40 on Monday night declares that he heard a heavy thud, as of a body striking the line, just before the train reached the station. There was dense fog, however, and nothing could be seen. He made no report of it at the time. Why, whatever is the matter with Mr. Holmes?"

My friend was standing with an expression of strained intensity upon his face, staring at the railway metals where they curved out of the tunnel. Aldgate is a junction, and there was a network of points. On these his eager, questioning eyes were fixed, and I saw on his keen, alert face that tightening of the lips, that quiver of the nostrils, and concentration of the heavy, tufted brows which I knew so well.

"Points," he muttered; "the points."

"What of it? What do you mean?"

"I suppose there are no great number of points on a system such as this?"

"No; they are very few."

"And a curve, too. Points, and a curve. By Jove! if it were only so."

"What is it, Mr. Holmes? Have you a clue?"

"An idea--an indication, no more. But the case certainly grows in interest. Unique, perfectly unique, and yet why not? I do not see any indications of bleeding on the line."

"There were hardly any."

"But I understand that there was a considerable wound."

"The bone was crushed, but there was no great external injury."

"And yet one would have expected some bleeding. Would it be possible for me to inspect the train which contained the passenger who heard the thud of a fall in the fog?"

"I fear not, Mr. Holmes. The train has been broken up before now, and the carriages redistributed."

"I can assure you, Mr. Holmes," said Lestrade, "that every carriage has been carefully examined. I saw to it myself."

It was one of my friend's most obvious weaknesses that he was impatient with less alert intelligences than his own.

"Very likely," said he, turning away. "As it happens, it was not the carriages which I desired to examine. Watson, we have done all we can here. We need not trouble you any further, Mr. Lestrade. I think our investigations must now carry us to Woolwich."

At London Bridge, Holmes wrote a telegram to his brother, which he handed to me before dispatching it. It ran thus:

```
See some light in the darkness, but it may
possibly flicker out. Meanwhile, please
send by messenger, to await return at Baker
Street, a complete list of all foreign
spies or international agents known to be
in England, with full address. Sherlock.
```

"That should be helpful, Watson," he remarked as we took our seats in the Woolwich train. "We certainly owe Brother Mycroft a debt for having introduced us to what promises to be a really very remarkable case."

His eager face still wore that expression of intense and high-strung energy, which showed me that some novel and suggestive circumstance had opened up a stimulating line of thought. See the foxhound with hanging ears and drooping tail as it lolls about the kennels, and compare it with the same hound as, with gleaming eyes and straining muscles, it runs upon a breast-high scent--such was the change in Holmes since the morning. He was a different man from the limp and lounging figure in the mouse-coloured dressing-gown who had prowled so restlessly only a few hours before round the fog-girt room.

"There is material here. There is scope," said he. "I am dull indeed not to have understood its possibilities."

"Even now they are dark to me."

"The end is dark to me also, but I have hold of one idea which may lead us far. The man met his death elsewhere, and his body was on the ROOF of a carriage."

"On the roof!"

"Remarkable, is it not? But consider the facts. Is it a coincidence that it is found at the very point where the train pitches and sways as it comes round on the points? Is not that the place where an object upon the roof might be expected to fall off? The points would affect no object inside the train. Either the body fell from the roof, or a very curious coincidence has occurred. But now consider the question of the blood. Of course, there was no bleeding on the line if the body had bled elsewhere. Each fact is suggestive in itself. Together they have a cumulative force."

"And the ticket, too!" I cried.

"Exactly. We could not explain the absence of a ticket. This would explain it. Everything fits together."

"But suppose it were so, we are still as far as ever from unravelling the mystery of his death. Indeed, it becomes not simpler but stranger."

"Perhaps," said Holmes, thoughtfully, "perhaps." He relapsed into a silent reverie, which lasted until the slow train drew up at last in Woolwich Station. There he called a cab and drew Mycroft's paper from his pocket.

"We have quite a little round of afternoon calls to make," said he. "I think that Sir James Walter claims our first attention."

The house of the famous official was a fine villa with green lawns stretching down to the Thames. As we reached it the fog was lifting, and a thin, watery sunshine was breaking through. A butler answered our ring.

"Sir James, sir!" said he with solemn face. "Sir James died this morning."

"Good heavens!" cried Holmes in amazement. "How did he die?"

"Perhaps you would care to step in, sir, and see his brother, Colonel Valentine?"

"Yes, we had best do so."

We were ushered into a dim-lit drawing-room, where an instant later we were joined by a very tall, handsome, light-beared man of fifty, the younger brother of the dead scientist. His wild eyes, stained cheeks, and unkempt hair all spoke of the sudden blow which had fallen upon the household. He was hardly articulate as he spoke of it.

"It was this horrible scandal," said he. "My brother, Sir James, was a man of very sensitive honour, and he could not survive such an affair. It broke his heart. He was always so proud of the efficiency of his department, and this was a crushing blow."

"We had hoped that he might have given us some indications which would have helped us to clear the matter up."

"I assure you that it was all a mystery to him as it is to you and to all of us. He had already put all his knowledge at the disposal of the police. Naturally he had no doubt that Cadogan West was guilty. But all the rest was inconceivable."

"You cannot throw any new light upon the affair?"

"I know nothing myself save what I have read or heard. I have no desire to be discourteous, but you can understand, Mr. Holmes, that we are much disturbed at present, and I must ask you to hasten this interview to an end."

"This is indeed an unexpected development," said my friend when we had regained the cab. "I wonder if the death was natural, or whether the poor old fellow killed himself! If the latter, may it be taken as some sign of self-reproach for duty neglected? We must leave that question to the future. Now we shall turn to the Cadogan Wests."

A small but well-kept house in the outskirts of the town sheltered the bereaved mother. The old lady was too dazed with grief to be of any use to us, but at her side was a white-faced young lady, who introduced herself as Miss Violet Westbury, the fiancee of the dead man, and the last to see him upon that fatal night.

"I cannot explain it, Mr. Holmes," she said. "I have not shut an eye since the tragedy, thinking, thinking, thinking, night and day, what the true meaning of it can be. Arthur was the most single-minded, chivalrous, patriotic man upon earth. He would have cut his right hand off before he would sell a State secret confided to his keeping. It is absurd, impossible, preposterous to anyone who knew him."

"But the facts, Miss Westbury?"

"Yes, yes; I admit I cannot explain them."

"Was he in any want of money?"

"No; his needs were very simple and his salary ample. He had saved a few hundreds, and we were to marry at the New Year."

"No signs of any mental excitement? Come, Miss Westbury, be absolutely frank with us."

The quick eye of my companion had noted some change in her manner. She coloured and hesitated.

"Yes," she said at last, "I had a feeling that there was something on his mind."

"For long?"

"Only for the last week or so. He was thoughtful and worried. Once I pressed him about it. He admitted that there was something, and that it was concerned with his official life. 'It is too serious for me to speak about, even to you,' said he. I could get nothing more."

Holmes looked grave.

"Go on, Miss Westbury. Even if it seems to tell against him, go on. We cannot say what it may lead to."

"Indeed, I have nothing more to tell. Once or twice it seemed to me that he was on the point of telling me something. He spoke one evening of the importance of the secret, and I have some recollection that he said that no doubt foreign spies would pay a great deal to have it."

My friend's face grew graver still.

"Anything else?"

"He said that we were slack about such matters--that it would be easy for a traitor to get the plans."

"Was it only recently that he made such remarks?"

"Yes, quite recently."

"Now tell us of that last evening."

"We were to go to the theatre. The fog was so thick that a cab was useless. We walked, and our way took us close to the office. Suddenly he darted away into the fog."

"Without a word?"

"He gave an exclamation; that was all. I waited but he never returned. Then I walked home. Next morning, after the office opened, they came to inquire. About twelve o'clock we heard the terrible news. Oh, Mr. Holmes, if you could only, only save his honour! It was so much to him."

Holmes shook his head sadly.

"Come, Watson," said he, "our ways lie elsewhere. Our next station must be the office from which the papers were taken.

"It was black enough before against this young man, but our inquiries make it blacker," he remarked as the cab lumbered off. "His coming marriage gives a motive for the crime. He naturally wanted money. The idea was in his head, since he spoke about it. He nearly made the girl an accomplice in the treason by telling her his plans. It is all very bad."

"But surely, Holmes, character goes for something? Then, again, why should he leave the girl in the street and dart away to commit a felony?"

"Exactly! There are certainly objections. But it is a formidable case which they have to meet."

Mr. Sidney Johnson, the senior clerk, met us at the office and received us with that respect which my companion's card always commanded. He was a thin, gruff, bespectacled man of middle age, his cheeks haggard, and his hands twitching from the nervous strain to which he had been subjected.

"It is bad, Mr. Holmes, very bad! Have you heard of the death of the chief?"

"We have just come from his house."

"The place is disorganized. The chief dead, Cadogan West dead, our papers stolen. And yet, when we closed our door on Monday evening, we were as efficient an office as any in the government service. Good God, it's dreadful to think of! That West, of all men, should have done such a thing!"

"You are sure of his guilt, then?"

"I can see no other way out of it. And yet I would have trusted him as I trust myself."

"At what hour was the office closed on Monday?"

"At five."

"Did you close it?"

"I am always the last man out."

"Where were the plans?"

"In that safe. I put them there myself."

"Is there no watchman to the building?"

"There is, but he has other departments to look after as well. He is an old soldier and a most trustworthy man. He saw nothing that evening. Of course the fog was very thick."

"Suppose that Cadogan West wished to make his way into the building after hours; he would need three keys, would he not, before he could reach the papers?"

"Yes, he would. The key of the outer door, the key of the office, and the key of the safe."

"Only Sir James Walter and you had those keys?"

"I had no keys of the doors--only of the safe."

"Was Sir James a man who was orderly in his habits?"

"Yes, I think he was. I know that so far as those three keys are concerned he kept them on the same ring. I have often seen them there."

"And that ring went with him to London?"

"He said so."

"And your key never left your possession?"

"Never."

"Then West, if he is the culprit, must have had a duplicate. And yet none was found upon his body. One other point: if a clerk in this office desired to sell the plans, would it not be simpler to copy the plans for himself than to take the originals, as was actually done?"

"It would take considerable technical knowledge to copy the plans in an effective way."

"But I suppose either Sir James, or you, or West has that technical knowledge?"

"No doubt we had, but I beg you won't try to drag me into the matter, Mr. Holmes. What is the use of our speculating in this way when the original plans were actually found on West?"

"Well, it is certainly singular that he should run the risk of taking originals if he could safely have taken copies, which would have equally served his turn."

"Singular, no doubt--and yet he did so."

"Every inquiry in this case reveals something inexplicable. Now there are three papers still missing. They are, as I understand, the vital ones."

"Yes, that is so."

"Do you mean to say that anyone holding these three papers, and without the seven others, could construct a Bruce-Partington submarine?"

"I reported to that effect to the Admiralty. But to-day I have been over the drawings again, and I am not so sure of it. The double valves with the automatic self-adjusting slots are drawn in one of the papers which have been returned. Until the foreigners had invented that for themselves they could not make the boat. Of course they might soon get over the difficulty."

"But the three missing drawings are the most important?"

"Undoubtedly."

"I think, with your permission, I will now take a stroll round the premises. I do not recall any other question which I desired to ask."

He examined the lock of the safe, the door of the room, and finally the iron shutters of the window. It was only when we were on the lawn outside that his interest was strongly excited. There was a laurel bush outside the window, and several of the branches bore signs of having been twisted or snapped. He examined them carefully with his lens, and then some dim and vague marks upon the earth beneath. Finally he asked the chief clerk to close the iron shutters, and he pointed out to me that they hardly met in the centre, and that it would be possible for anyone outside to see what was going on within the room.

"The indications are ruined by three days' delay. They may mean something or nothing. Well, Watson, I do not think that Woolwich can help us further. It is a small crop which we have gathered. Let us see if we can do better in London."

Yet we added one more sheaf to our harvest before we left Woolwich Station. The clerk in the ticket office was able to say with confidence that he saw Cadogan West--whom he knew well by sight-- upon the Monday night, and that he went to London by the 8:15 to London Bridge. He was alone and took a single third-class ticket. The clerk was struck at the time by his excited and nervous manner. So shaky was he that he could hardly pick up his change, and the clerk had helped him with it. A reference to the timetable showed that the 8:15 was the first train which it was possible for West to take after he had left the lady about 7:30.

"Let us reconstruct, Watson," said Holmes after half an hour of silence. "I am not aware that in all our joint researches we have ever had a case which was more difficult to get at. Every fresh advance which we make only reveals a fresh ridge beyond. And yet we have surely made some appreciable progress.

"The effect of our inquiries at Woolwich has in the main been against young Cadogan West; but the indications at the window would lend themselves to a more favourable hypothesis. Let us suppose, for example, that he had been approached by some foreign agent. It might have been done under such pledges as would have prevented him from speaking of it, and yet would have affected his thoughts in the direction indicated by his remarks to his fiancee. Very good. We will now suppose that as he went to the theatre with the young lady he suddenly, in the fog, caught a glimpse of this same agent going in the direction of the office. He was an impetuous man, quick in his decisions. Everything gave way to his duty. He followed the man, reached the window, saw the abstraction of the documents, and pursued the thief. In this way we get over the objection that no one would take originals when he could make copies. This outsider had to take originals. So far it holds together."

"What is the next step?"

"Then we come into difficulties. One would imagine that under such circumstances the first act of young Cadogan West would be to seize the villain and raise the alarm. Why did he not do so? Could it have been an official superior who took the papers? That would explain West's conduct. Or could the chief have given West the slip in the fog, and West started at once to London to head him off from his own rooms, presuming that he knew where the rooms were? The call must have been very pressing, since he left his girl standing in the fog and made no effort to communicate with her. Our scent runs cold here, and there is a vast gap between either hypothesis and the laying of West's body, with seven papers in his pocket, on the roof of a Metropolitan train. My instinct now is to work from the other end. If Mycroft has given us the list of addresses we may be able to pick our man and follow two tracks instead of one."

Surely enough, a note awaited us at Baker Street. A government messenger had brought it post-haste. Holmes glanced at it and threw it over to me.

There are numerous small fry, but few who would handle so big an affair. The only men worth considering are Adolph Mayer, of 13 Great George Street, Westminster; Louis La Rothiere, of Campden Mansions, Notting Hill; and Hugo Oberstein, 13 Caulfield Gardens, Kensington. The latter was known to be in town on Monday and is now reported as having left. Glad to hear you have seen some light. The Cabinet awaits your final report with the utmost anxiety. Urgent representations have arrived from the very highest quarter. The whole force of the State is at your back if you should need it.

Mycroft.

"I'm afraid," said Holmes, smiling, "that all the queen's horses and all the queen's men cannot avail in this matter." He had spread out his big map of London and leaned eagerly over it. "Well, well," said he presently with an exclamation of satisfaction, "things are turning a little in our direction at last. Why, Watson, I do honestly believe that we are going to pull it off, after all." He slapped me on the shoulder with a sudden burst of hilarity. "I am going out now. It is only a reconnaissance. I will do nothing serious without my trusted comrade and biographer at my elbow. Do you stay here, and the odds are that you will see me again in an hour or two. If time hangs heavy get foolscap and a pen, and begin your narrative of how we saved the State."

I felt some reflection of his elation in my own mind, for I knew well that he would not depart so far from his usual austerity of demeanour unless there was good cause for exultation. All the long November evening I waited, filled with impatience for his return. At last, shortly after nine o'clock, there arrived a messenger with a note:

Am dining at Goldini's Restaurant, Gloucester Road, Kensington. Please come at once and join me there. Bring with you a jemmy, a dark lantern, a chisel, and a revolver. S.H.

It was a nice equipment for a respectable citizen to carry through the dim, fog-draped streets. I stowed them all discreetly away in my overcoat and drove straight to the address given. There sat my friend at a little round table near the door of the garish Italian restaurant.

"Have you had something to eat? Then join me in a coffee and curacao. Try one of the proprietor's cigars. They are less poisonous than one would expect. Have you the tools?"

"They are here, in my overcoat."

"Excellent. Let me give you a short sketch of what I have done, with some indication of what we are about to do. Now it must be evident to you, Watson, that this young man's body was PLACED on the roof of the train. That was clear from the instant that I determined the fact that it was from the roof, and not from a carriage, that he had fallen."

"Could it not have been dropped from a bridge?"

"I should say it was impossible. If you examine the roofs you will find that they are slightly rounded, and there is no railing round them. Therefore, we can say for certain that young Cadogan West was placed on it."

"How could he be placed there?"

"That was the question which we had to answer. There is only one possible way. You are aware that the Underground runs clear of tunnels at some points in the West End. I had a vague memory that as I have travelled by it I have occasionally seen windows just above my head. Now, suppose that a train halted under such a window, would there be any difficulty in laying a body upon the roof?"

"It seems most improbable."

"We must fall back upon the old axiom that when all other contingencies fail, whatever remains, however improbable, must be the truth. Here all other contingencies HAVE failed. When I found that the leading international agent, who had just left London, lived in a row of houses which abutted upon the Underground, I was so pleased that you were a little astonished at my sudden frivolity."

"Oh, that was it, was it?"

"Yes, that was it. Mr. Hugo Oberstein, of 13 Caulfield Gardens, had become my objective. I began my operations at Gloucester Road Station, where a very helpful official walked with me along the track and allowed me to satisfy myself not only that the back-stair windows of Caulfield Gardens open on the line but the even more essential fact that, owing to the intersection of one of the larger railways, the Underground trains are frequently held motionless for some minutes at that very spot."

"Splendid, Holmes! You have got it!"

"So far--so far, Watson. We advance, but the goal is afar. Well, having seen the back of Caulfield Gardens, I visited the front and satisfied myself that the bird was indeed flown. It is a considerable house, unfurnished, so far as I could judge, in the upper rooms. Oberstein lived there with a single valet, who was probably a confederate entirely in his confidence. We must bear in mind that Oberstein has gone to the Continent to dispose of his booty, but not with any idea of flight; for he had no reason to fear a warrant, and the idea of an amateur domiciliary visit would certainly never occur to him. Yet that is precisely what we are about to make."

"Could we not get a warrant and legalize it?"

"Hardly on the evidence."

"What can we hope to do?"

"We cannot tell what correspondence may be there."

"I don't like it, Holmes."

"My dear fellow, you shall keep watch in the street. I'll do the criminal part. It's not a time to stick at trifles. Think of Mycroft's note, of the Admiralty, the Cabinet, the exalted person who waits for news. We are bound to go."

My answer was to rise from the table.

"You are right, Holmes. We are bound to go."

He sprang up and shook me by the hand.

"I knew you would not shrink at the last," said he, and for a moment I saw something in his eyes which was nearer to tenderness than I had ever seen. The next instant he was his masterful, practical self once more.

"It is nearly half a mile, but there is no hurry. Let us walk," said he. "Don't drop the instruments, I beg. Your arrest as a suspicious character would be a most unfortunate complication."

Caulfield Gardens was one of those lines of flat-faced pillared, and porticoed houses which are so prominent a product of the middle Victorian epoch in the West End of London. Next door there appeared to be a children's party, for the merry buzz of young voices and the clatter of a piano resounded through the night. The fog still hung about and screened us with its friendly shade. Holmes had lit his lantern and flashed it upon the massive door.

"This is a serious proposition," said he. "It is certainly bolted as well as locked. We would do better in the area. There is an excellent archway down yonder in case a too zealous policeman should intrude. Give me a hand, Watson, and I'll do the same for you."

A minute later we were both in the area. Hardly had we reached the dark shadows before the step of the policeman was heard in the fog above. As its soft rhythm died away, Holmes set to work upon the lower door. I saw him stoop and strain until with a sharp crash it flew open. We sprang through into the dark passage, closing the area door behind us. Holmes led the way up the curving, uncarpeted stair. His little fan of yellow light shone upon a low window.

"Here we are, Watson--this must be the one." He threw it open, and as he did so there was a low, harsh murmur, growing steadily into a loud roar as a train dashed past us in the darkness. Holmes swept his light along the window-sill. It was thickly coated with soot from the passing engines, but the black surface was blurred and rubbed in places.

"You can see where they rested the body. Halloa, Watson! what is this? There can be no doubt that it is a blood mark." He was pointing to faint discolourations along the woodwork of the window. "Here it is on the stone of the stair also. The demonstration is complete. Let us stay here until a train stops."

We had not long to wait. The very next train roared from the tunnel as before, but slowed in the open, and then, with a creaking of brakes, pulled up immediately beneath us. It was not four feet from the window-ledge to the roof of the carriages. Holmes softly closed the window.

"So far we are justified," said he. "What do you think of it, Watson?"

"A masterpiece. You have never risen to a greater height."

"I cannot agree with you there. From the moment that I conceived the idea of the body being upon the roof, which surely was not a very abstruse one, all the rest was inevitable. If it were not for the grave interests involved the affair up to this point would be insignificant. Our difficulties are still before us. But perhaps we may find something here which may help us."

We had ascended the kitchen stair and entered the suite of rooms upon the first floor. One was a dining-room, severely furnished and containing nothing of interest. A second was a bedroom, which also drew blank. The remaining room appeared more promising, and my companion settled down to a systematic examination. It was littered with books and papers, and was evidently used as a study. Swiftly and methodically Holmes turned over the contents of drawer after drawer and cupboard after cupboard, but no gleam of success came to brighten his austere face. At the end of an hour he was no further than when he started.

"The cunning dog has covered his tracks," said he. "He has left nothing to incriminate him. His dangerous correspondence has been destroyed or removed. This is our last chance."

It was a small tin cash-box which stood upon the writing-desk. Holmes pried it open with his chisel. Several rolls of paper were within, covered with figures and calculations, without any note to show to what they referred. The recurring words, "water pressure" and "pressure to the square inch" suggested some possible relation to a submarine. Holmes tossed them all impatiently aside. There only remained an envelope with some small newspaper slips inside it. He shook them out on the table, and at once I saw by his eager face that his hopes had been raised.

"What's this, Watson? Eh? What's this? Record of a series of messages in the advertisements of a paper. Daily Telegraph agony column by the print and paper. Right-hand top corner of a page. No dates--but messages arrange themselves. This must be the first:

"Hoped to hear sooner. Terms agreed to. Write fully to address given on card.

"Pierrot.

"Next comes:

"Too complex for description. Must have full report, Stuff awaits you when goods delivered.

"Pierrot.

"Then comes:

"Matter presses. Must withdraw offer unless contract completed. Make appointment by letter. Will confirm by advertisement.

"Pierrot.

"Finally:

"Monday night after nine. Two taps. Only
ourselves. Do not be so suspicious.
Payment in hard cash when goods delivered.

"Pierrot.

"A fairly complete record, Watson! If we could only get at the man at the other end!" He sat lost in thought, tapping his fingers on the table. Finally he sprang to his feet.

"Well, perhaps it won't be so difficult, after all. There is nothing more to be done here, Watson. I think we might drive round to the offices of the Daily Telegraph, and so bring a good day's work to a conclusion."

Mycroft Holmes and Lestrade had come round by appointment after breakfast next day and Sherlock Holmes had recounted to them our proceedings of the day before. The professional shook his head over our confessed burglary.

"We can't do these things in the force, Mr. Holmes," said he. "No wonder you get results that are beyond us. But some of these days you'll go too far, and you'll find yourself and your friend in trouble."

"For England, home and beauty--eh, Watson? Martyrs on the altar of our country. But what do you think of it, Mycroft?"

"Excellent, Sherlock! Admirable! But what use will you make of it?"

Holmes picked up the Daily Telegraph which lay upon the table.

"Have you seen Pierrot's advertisement to-day?"

"What? Another one?"

"Yes, here it is:

"To-night. Same hour. Same place. Two
taps. Most vitally important. Your own
safety at stake.

"Pierrot.

"By George!" cried Lestrade. "If he answers that we've got him!"

"That was my idea when I put it in. I think if you could both make it convenient to come with us about eight o'clock to Caulfield Gardens we might possibly get a little nearer to a solution."

One of the most remarkable characteristics of Sherlock Holmes was his power of throwing his brain out of action and switching all his thoughts on to lighter things whenever he had convinced himself that he could no longer work to advantage. I remember that during the whole of that memorable day he lost himself in a monograph which he had undertaken upon the Polyphonic Motets of Lassus. For my own part I had none of this power of detachment, and the day, in consequence, appeared to be interminable. The great national importance of the issue, the suspense in high quarters, the direct nature of the experiment which we were trying--all combined to work upon my nerve. It was a relief to me when at last, after a light dinner, we set out upon our expedition. Lestrade and Mycroft met us by appointment at the outside of Gloucester Road Station. The area door of Oberstein's house had been left open the night before, and it was necessary for me, as Mycroft Holmes absolutely and indignantly declined to climb the railings, to pass in and open the hall door. By nine o'clock we were all seated in the study, waiting patiently for our man.

An hour passed and yet another. When eleven struck, the measured beat of the great church clock seemed to sound the dirge of our hopes. Lestrade and Mycroft were fidgeting in their seats and looking twice a minute at their watches. Holmes sat silent and composed, his eyelids half shut, but every sense on the alert. He raised his head with a sudden jerk.

"He is coming," said he.

There had been a furtive step past the door. Now it returned. We heard a shuffling sound outside, and then two sharp taps with the knocker. Holmes rose, motioning us to remain seated. The gas in the hall was a mere point of light. He opened the outer door, and then as a dark figure slipped past him he closed and fastened it. "This way!" we heard him say, and a moment later our man stood before us.

Holmes had followed him closely, and as the man turned with a cry of surprise and alarm he caught him by the collar and threw him back into the room. Before our prisoner had recovered his balance the door was shut and Holmes standing with his back against it. The man glared round him, staggered, and fell senseless upon the floor. With the shock, his broad-brimmed hat flew from his head, his cravat slipped down from his lips, and there were the long light beard and the soft, handsome delicate features of Colonel Valentine Walter.

Holmes gave a whistle of surprise.

"You can write me down an ass this time, Watson," said he. "This was not the bird that I was looking for."

"Who is he?" asked Mycroft eagerly.

"The younger brother of the late Sir James Walter, the head of the Submarine Department. Yes, yes; I see the fall of the cards. He is coming to. I think that you had best leave his examination to me."

We had carried the prostrate body to the sofa. Now our prisoner sat up, looked round him with a horror-stricken face, and passed his hand over his forehead, like one who cannot believe his own senses.

"What is this?" he asked. "I came here to visit Mr. Oberstein."

"Everything is known, Colonel Walter," said Holmes. "How an English gentleman could behave in such a manner is beyond my comprehension. But your whole correspondence and relations with Oberstein are within our knowledge. So also are the circumstances connected with the death of young Cadogan West. Let me advise you to gain at least the small credit for repentance and confession, since there are still some details which we can only learn from your lips."

The man groaned and sank his face in his hands. We waited, but he was silent.

"I can assure you," said Holmes, "that every essential is already known. We know that you were pressed for money; that you took an impress of the keys which your brother held; and that you entered into a correspondence with Oberstein, who answered your letters through the advertisement columns of the Daily Telegraph. We are aware that you went down to the office in the fog on Monday night, but that you were seen and followed by young Cadogan West, who had probably some previous reason to suspect you. He saw your theft, but could not give the alarm, as it was just possible that you were taking the papers to your brother in London. Leaving all his private concerns, like the good citizen that he was, he followed you closely in the fog and kept at your heels until you reached this very house. There he intervened, and then it was, Colonel Walter, that to treason you added the more terrible crime of murder."

"I did not! I did not! Before God I swear that I did not!" cried our wretched prisoner.

"Tell us, then, how Cadogan West met his end before you laid him upon the roof of a railway carriage."

"I will. I swear to you that I will. I did the rest. I confess it. It was just as you say. A Stock Exchange debt had to be paid. I needed the money badly. Oberstein offered me five thousand. It was to save myself from ruin. But as to murder, I am as innocent as you."

"What happened, then?"

"He had his suspicions before, and he followed me as you describe. I never knew it until I was at the very door. It was thick fog, and one could not see three yards. I had given two taps and Oberstein had come to the door. The young man rushed up and demanded to know what we were about to do with the papers. Oberstein had a short life-preserver. He always carried it with him. As West forced his way after us into the house Oberstein struck him on the head. The blow was a fatal one. He was dead within five minutes. There he lay in the hall, and we were at our wit's end what to do. Then Oberstein had this idea about the trains which halted under his back window. But first he examined the papers which I had brought. He said that three of them were essential, and that he must keep them. 'You cannot keep them,' said I. 'There will be a dreadful row at Woolwich if they are not returned.' 'I must keep them,' said he, 'for they are so technical that it is impossible in the time to make copies.' 'Then they must all go back together to-night,' said I. He thought for a little, and then he cried out that he had it. 'Three I will keep,' said he. 'The others we will stuff into the pocket of this young man. When he is found the whole business will assuredly be put to his account.' I could see no other way out of it, so we did as he suggested. We waited half an hour at the window before a train stopped. It was so thick that nothing could be seen, and we had no difficulty in lowering West's body on to the train. That was the end of the matter so far as I was concerned."

"And your brother?"

"He said nothing, but he had caught me once with his keys, and I think that he suspected. I read in his eyes that he suspected. As you know, he never held up his head again."

There was silence in the room. It was broken by Mycroft Holmes.

"Can you not make reparation? It would ease your conscience, and possibly your punishment."

"What reparation can I make?"

"Where is Oberstein with the papers?"

"I do not know."

"Did he give you no address?"

"He said that letters to the Hotel du Louvre, Paris, would eventually reach him."

"Then reparation is still within your power," said Sherlock Holmes.

"I will do anything I can. I owe this fellow no particular good-will. He has been my ruin and my downfall."

"Here are paper and pen. Sit at this desk and write to my dictation. Direct the envelope to the address given. That is right. Now the letter:

```
Dear Sir:
```

"With regard to our transaction, you will no doubt have observed by now that one essential detail is missing. I have a tracing which will make it complete. This has involved me in extra trouble, however, and I must ask you for a further advance of five hundred pounds. I will not trust it to the post, nor will I take anything but gold or notes. I would come to you abroad, but it would excite remark if I left the

```
country at present. Therefore I shall
expect to meet you in the smoking-room of
the Charing Cross Hotel at noon on
Saturday. Remember that only English notes,
or gold, will be taken.
```

"That will do very well. I shall be very much surprised if it does not fetch our man."

And it did! It is a matter of history--that secret history of a nation which is often so much more intimate and interesting than its public chronicles--that Oberstein, eager to complete the coup of his lifetime, came to the lure and was safely engulfed for fifteen years in a British prison. In his trunk were found the invaluable Bruce-Partington plans, which he had put up for auction in all the naval centres of Europe.

Colonel Walter died in prison towards the end of the second year of his sentence. As to Holmes, he returned refreshed to his monograph upon the Polyphonic Motets of Lassus, which has since been printed for private circulation, and is said by experts to be the last word upon the subject. Some weeks afterwards I learned incidentally that my friend spent a day at Windsor, whence he returned with a remarkably fine emerald tie-pin. When I asked him if he had bought it, he answered that it was a present from a certain gracious lady in whose interests he had once been fortunate enough to carry out a small commission. He said no more; but I fancy that I could guess at that lady's august name, and I have little doubt that the emerald pin will forever recall to my friend's memory the adventure of the Bruce-Partington plans.

Made in the USA
Middletown, DE
12 February 2021